CHOSEN BY A STREET KING

K. RENEE AND LATOYA NICOLE

AKNOWLEDGMENTS

OVER THE LAST FEW MONTHS, WE HAVE GOTTEN A MILLION REQUESTS FOR US TO COLLAB TOGETHER. YOU ASKED AND WE DELIVERED. THANK YOU FROM THE BOTTOM OF OUR HEARTS FOR ALWAYS SUPPORTING US, PUSHING US, AND MOST OF ALL BRINGING TWO DOPE WRITERS TOGETHER. WITHOUT YOU ALL, NONE OF THIS WAS POSSIBLE. MAKE SURE YOU CHECK OUT OUR OTHER BOOKS LISTED AT THE END OF THE BOOK.

Special birthday shout outs to our readers. Happy bday Tiffany Polnitz, Anesha Davis, Terris Burney, Dominique Rochelle- Jones, Latoya Backie, Roshema Batiste, London Shaw, Camille b Nurse.

SYNOPSIS...

After their father decided to retire and pass the reigns down to his sons Mega, Meech, and Marco. The three took over Philly by storm. With Mega leading the pack, the brothers found themselves bringing in more money than their father ever did, but it also brought in more enemies. The Storm brothers are considered the plug to the streets, so love was never on their agenda. Having their fair share, neither Mega nor Meech were worried about women until they stumbled upon two sisters by chance.

An unexpected incident caused Mega and Brielle to cross paths, and they hit it off right away. Things seem to be going great, until old relationships and secrets started to tear them apart.

Hurt by love, Meech has sworn off relationships. All seemed lost when it came to him finding love, until Dream fought her way into his life. Literally. Their love hate relationship drew them closer, until family ties and assumptions had Meech going back to his old ways.

In trying to prove his family wrong, Marco stays with his longtime girlfriend after giving herself to another. Fighting for love, all while trying to find happiness with a woman he no longer trusts, eventually comes to an end. The ultimate betrayal with a sworn enemy puts all the brother's lives at risk.

Every time the Storm brothers tackle one enemy, it seems like another comes at them full force. All of them seemed to not only be connected to each other, but also to the people they love the most. Will they trust the people around them, or will they declare war on everyone in their circle?

3

Megillian "Mega" Storm...

I'm sitting here listening to these bitch niggas feed me some bullshit on why the fuck my money is missing! It was damn near five in the morning, and I had to leave my damn bed to deal with these stupid mufuckas. I was a cranky nigga, especially when my damn sleep is interrupted with dumb shit.

"How fuckin' much?" I didn't have time to sit and listen to this long, drawn-out fuckin' shit. All I needed to know is how much of my fuckin' money was gone.

"It was three hundred, but that shit wasn't our fault!" This nigga Kyle, had the nerve to say.

"Bitch, when my money is fuckin' missing, and you're the mufucka that got hit up, nigga I expect you to guard that shit with yo muthafuckin' life! Don't come up in here talking that it's not my fault shit. That lets me know it's yo fuckin' fault." He had me fucked up.

"Bruh, it still wasn't our fault. I mean, I hear what the fuck you say-" I cut that nigga off with a shot to the head. A few things I don't fuck around with, and that's my money, my mama, and my muthafuckin' peace!

"Dammmnnnn, nigga! This the type shit you on? I should've left yo grumpy ass sleep. You can't even ask the nigga what happened now, because he fuckin' dead." Marco shook his head as he looked at me in disbelief.

"Do it look like I give a fuck! This nigga Shawn gone work off the debt, or he gone die off that mufucka," I spoke, just as our brother Meech came walking in.

"I had to slide out of some good ass pussy, what the fuck these niggas do?" He asked with a mug on his face.

"Got hit for three hundred racks." I could barely say that shit.

"How the fuck that happen?" He asked no one in particular, and Shawn shrugged his shoulders. Shit had me wondering if that nigga Lenox had something to do with it. He never did anything off, but the nigga rubbed me wrong. The only reason his ass was still alive, because pops said I was acting light skinned. As long as the nigga was buying product, I had no reason to be at his head. I let his ass make it, but the first time I think his ass on some grimy shit, I'mma put that bitch ass nigga to sleep.

When pops ran the city, he had his hand in everything. Nigga was selling dope, running numbers, hoes, and anything else you could think of. I wasn't trying to run my shit how his ass did, so I shook some shit up. Instead of trying to pimp bitches, I opened a strip club called Haze and let them get they money that way. It brought in more bread and they were able to keep all profits if they chose to sell pussy. We only did bets on legitimate shit, like fights and games. Of course, our biggest profit was from drugs.

We had a good connect and we got that shit dirt cheap. Mufuckas loved our product, so they wanted in. We sold that shit for twice the amount we paid for it. My pops hated that I did that shit better than him, and his ass stayed beefing with me for it. I loved letting his ass know shit was good. You would think he was old as hell the way he wanted to run shit. His ass was only forty-nine. Outside of his looks and age, that nigga acted as if he was seventy.

"I want my money; you got sixty days! If I don't get my shit, I'm killing yo bitch ass next." That was the last thing I said as I turned to leave.

"How you gon' leave and you got this dead nigga lying here on the floor?" Marco was doing that baby bullshit.

"Take care of it. I'm going back to bed." I was tired as hell.

"I'm not cleaning that nigga up. I got pussy waiting on me." Meech laughed and followed me out.

"Y'all some straight bitches for that shit! I can't wait until we get to dinner tonight, I'm telling Ma on y'all punk asses!" Marco yelled out behind us, and that halted our steps. Our mama Talia, was no fuckin' joke, and she didn't play no games about her boys. Marco was her baby, and she went extra hard over his snitching ass. Our pop Maine, didn't care what the fuck we did as long as he got his fuckin' money every month. Both of our parents were in the game back in the day, and they ass still acted as if they were out there in the streets.

When my mom got pregnant with me, my pop let her know that her slangin' and bangin' days were over. When I turned eighteen, I started working for my pops. Five years ago, Pops said he was retiring and turned everything over to us. He put me in charge, and my brothers were by my side. I'm twenty-nine years old, my brother Meech is twenty-six, and Marco is twenty-four. I was the deadliest, but I thought things through no matter what the issue was. Meech... that nigga was crazy, disrespectful, and will kill you without a thought. Marco always looked to me before he made any moves. He never acted off impulse, but if he's pushed you most definitely gon' die.

"I swear one of these days I'm going to beat the shit out of his ass!" Meech went off as he dialed the cleanup crew.

"Just let me know when and where. I want in on that shit. I got years of aggression to let off on his ass," I told Meech as we both bust out laughing.

"Ohhhh, I see you two niggas came back to join me." Marco bitch ass smirked, and I wanted to knock that shit off his face.

"Nigga, shut yo dumb ass up!" Meech was talking shit and I didn't blame him. It took about two hours for them to clean up the mess I made. I was now in my car and on my way back home. When I pulled in the garage, this chick came out of nowhere, and I slammed on my brakes, but it was too late; I had already hit her. I jumped out of my car, and she was on the ground holding her leg in tears.

"Yo what the fuck? Are you alright lil mama?" I asked her as I bent down to check her out.

"No, I have a lot of pain in my leg," she whimpered. I hoped her shit wasn't broken.

"I think you need to get this checked out. I'm going to lift you up and put you in my car."

"No! I don't know you! What the fuck is wrong with you, you could have killed me!" This smart mouth ass chick was trying to go off and I wasn't in the mood for her shit. Low key, it wasn't my fault and I wasn't about to deal with her attitude too much longer.

"You jumped out in front of my damn car; I wasn't driving that fast. If you would have been paying the fuck attention to where you were going, instead of being on your phone, you wouldn't have gotten hit. The fuck you talkin' bout!" I know I was going off, but this chick got me fuckin' heated.

"Just give me your insurance information, and I will deal with you later," she spat.

"Deal with me? Bit..." I had to catch myself. I tried not to be disrespectful to women, but this chick was pushing it. "Bruh, there is not a muthafuckin' soul on earth that will deal with me. I will pay for your medical bills only because I feel bad. Not because you think you're going to deal with me!"

"Bruh! Who the fuck are you calling bruh? Do I look like a dude to you?" She questioned mad as hell. I didn't really give a damn about her attitude. I went to my car and grabbed something to write my number down.

"Here is my number lil mama. Just let me know what my bill is gonna be, and I will handle that shit." Leaving her with that, I walked back to my car and pulled into my parking spot. Going into my penthouse, I couldn't get the chick out of my mind. I don't know if it was her feisty attitude or her beauty that was fuckin' with me.

She had these big curls that bounced all over her head, as she moved back and forth talking her shit. I was a sucker for a big ass and wide hips, and trust me, lil mama had everything that I was looking for. She wasn't your regular slim chick; she was thick and sexy just the way I liked it. The fuck was I gon' do with a small chick that I could hold with one hand. I would fuck around and snap her lil ass in two.

I had nothing against small women; they just weren't my cup of tea. I'm not saying lil mama was a big girl, which I have dated my share of. She was just a thick girl with some love handles for my ass to grip up. It was something about her that I couldn't shake, but I needed to. She had a smart-ass mouth, and I can't deal with a chick like that.

I crawled back in bed, and minutes later, I was out like a light. My phone was going off, and that shit pissed me off. "**Fucccck!**" I roared out loud. Grabbing my phone, it was a number I didn't recognize. I decided to answer the call just in case it was one of my brothers.

"Yeah."

"My bill is a little over thirteen hundred dollars. You broke my leg, and I have to be in a cast for six weeks. I'm going to miss days from work, and I need my fuckin' money!" She was yelling, so I hung up on her ass. I don't know who the fuck she thought she was talking to, but lil mama got the wrong nigga. She called back again, but I ignored that shit and turned my phone off. I will call her ass when I'm ready to fuckin' talk!

Demetrius "Meech" Storm

"Ma said bring yo slow ass over here. She didn't cook all this food for you to stand her up." Marco bitch ass was getting on my nerves. He was a straight mama's boy and that shit was mad annoying. His ass needed to grow the fuck up.

"Bruh, I'm balls deep in some pussy right now. I'll be there when I'm done. Talia only cares about you being there anyway, fuck you calling me for?" Not waiting for an answer, I hung up the phone. Looking back at the bitch I had bent over; I went back to work in her pussy. "Arch yo back or something." Shit was stiff as hell.

"I am. What you want me to do, break it?" Her ass was whining, and it was irritating.

"Fuck yeah, if that's what it takes for you to get that shit right. Feel like I'm fucking the headboard. Bend this shit, damn." Smacking her lips, she did a move like her ass was doing what I asked. Instead, she ended up looking like she had a humpback. I didn't know it was possible for the shit to get worst.

"This hurts. Can I just get on top?" I wanted to put the hoe out, but my dick was harder than yesterday's booger.

"Come on." Climbing on top, this mufucka started doing that old lady scoot, and I was over this shit already. "You about to bend my dick. Hop on this bitch or something." Doing as I suggested, she started bouncing that ass, and that was better. Closing my eyes, I allowed her to take over. Shit was feeling good, and I thought I was about to cum, until I felt her fly off my dick. Opening my eyes, all I saw was Talia punching the girl in her mouth.

"You think I cooked all that food for you to stand me the fuck up. Get yo slow ass up and put yo fucking clothes on." This lady was batshit crazy.

"Me and my girl was busy man. I'll be over in a few." Looking at me like I was crazy, she shook her head.

"What's her name Meech?" I tried to look over to the slow ass hoe for her to give me a clue, but her dumb ass just looked at me. I had a good mind to take her in my back room.

"It don't matter what her name is. This shit is ridiculous."

"I'm not going to tell you again. Get dressed while I drag this hoe up out of here. Get yo slow ass up and come on." Talia didn't give me a chance to protest. She dragged the girl down the stairs naked and all. Grabbing my jogging pants, I slid them on when Talia walked back in and smacked the shit out of me. "I know you don't think you about to sit at my table smelling like ass and skid marks and teach that child how to ride. Shit was pitiful. Go get yo dumb ass in the shower and wash that bitch off. Thank you."

"Can you get the fuck out of my house, damn?"

"Nope, I sure can't." Her ass sat down in the chair and looked at my bed in disgust.

"If you gone be here, at least go feed Lana for me." She looked at me like I lost my mind.

"I'm not going back there with that thing. What am I supposed to feed it, my arm? I'm good." Laughing, I walked in the bathroom.

"I keep telling y'all she a vegetarian." Lana was my baby tiger, and everyone acted as if she was a danger to society. That was my child and the only one I planned on having. I paid a lot of money to get her, and I had her since she was nine weeks old. My lil mama was not mean or a danger, they ass was just a bunch of hoes.

"That's yo plan? To feed her grass and shit hoping she won't eat yo dumb ass. Whew, I raised a bunch of dumb mufuckas. Hurry up and wash yo ass. If all Lana is eating is grass, the bitch might bust through the door and eat me alive. You know it's some lesbian animals out here too, and I got good pussy." Talia started looking around and shit as if my baby was trying to get her. Ignoring her, I jumped in the shower and washed my ass.

When I got out, I got dressed in the bathroom since she was still sitting in the room waiting on me. Shaking my head when I walked out, I grabbed my shoes and slid them on. Even though Marco was the baby, and she spoiled him rotten, my mama didn't play about her kids. I talked shit to her, but deep down, I was her favorite. Mufuckas couldn't tell me different.

"You know I'm driving my own car, right? I didn't need you to wait on me."

"Nigga please. I can't trust you. If I had left, yo ass would have called the lil bitch right back. Besides, didn't I tell you it's not cool to play where you lay? You don't know these hoes, and I'm sick of you trusting them in yo shit." She shook her head as we walked out the door, but I think she forgot about my daughter.

"Talia, who gone try something with Lana in the next room? I got this, just make sure I got a full stomach after I empty my balls and we good. That's all I need you to do." Shooting me a death look, she got in her car and drove off. I couldn't do shit but laugh as I did the same. Since I saw she was in her Porsche, and I was in my Bugatti, I took off like we were in a race. As soon as she realized what I was doing, she hit the gas and tried to catch up. I was ghosting her for about fifteen minutes, until a police car came out of nowhere. Irritated, I put my gun up and pulled over. When I saw the officer that was coming up to my window, I shook my head.

"Jim, why the fuck are you pulling me over?" It was a cop that was on my pop's payroll, and he knew my car. And if he didn't, he realized it when he ran my plates.

"I'm sorry Meech, your mother called and told me to. She said she needed you off the road for like five minutes." Seeing her fly past me laughing, it took everything in me not to shoot out her tires. His weak ass actually stood in front of my car so I couldn't pull off. Five minutes later, he was moving. "Have a good day, sir."

Not even responding, I took off like a bat out of hell. I tried my best to catch up, but by the time I got to my parent's house, she was walking in the front door after she stuck up her middle finger first. Getting out, I rushed inside.

"You a cheating big-headed hoe. Why you had to call Jim to win?" Before I could say anything else, I got punched in the ear. Turning around, I saw it was my pops and bit my tongue.

"Don't talk to my wife like that. I'mma need you to remember who the fuck that is. Now go wash yo hands and get ready to eat." When I saw Marco laugh, I walked past him, drew my leg back and kicked him in the nuts.

"Maaaa!" he screamed in a pained voice.

"I swear all you do is snitch." When Talia walked in and saw him hurled over in pain, I ran in the bathroom and closed the door. Making sure it was locked, I sat on the toilet for about ten minutes trying to buy me some time. This was my life since as long as I could remember. Marco has never fought a battle on his own. I remember one time when we were kids, some lil nigga from the hood called his ass out to fight. We all stood around and let them go head-on. Lil nigga was whooping Marco's ass while we all laughed and took bets. Talia came out of nowhere and knocked the lil mufucka out. When we got home, she beat our ass for allowing him to get whooped. Said if we ever allowed that shit to happen again, she would shoot us. Washing my hands, I opened the door, and a shoe came flying in, hitting me in the face.

"Scary bitch, come eat." When Talia walked off, I mugged the shit out of Marco. I was gone get his ass. Nigga thought shit was sweet, but his time was coming.

Demarco "Marco" Storm

I was going to pay Meech ass back for that nut shot. Nigga was always playing, but I couldn't lie, I loved that shit. One thing about me and my brothers, we go in on each other, but there isn't a nigga alive that could fuck with one of us.

"Punk ass nigga, always getting me into some shit with Talia," Meech gritted on me, but I bet his punk ass wasn't gonna hit me again.

"Nigga, you should keep yo feet to yourself. The next time you do that shit I'mma shoot you and have Mega feed you to that lil bitch you got over there at yo crib. That shit doesn't even seem safe. That's why I don't visit yo ass. Ion want no parts of that lil ugly bitch." I looked at him with a mug on my face.

"Keep fuckin' with me, and I'm gone make sure you two meet sooner than later. She already knows you a scary ass nigga anyway." He laughed, and I stuck my middle finger up at his ass.

"Ma, how is it that you came and harassed me while I was knee deep, but you just let Mega do what the hell he wants to do? Why you ain't run up in his shit? You got a key to all of our shit, so don't say you couldn't get in," Meech said to her, and Ma went the fuck off.

"Mind the business that pays you, nigga. I do what I want, when the fuck I want to, and tonight I wanted to fuck with yo hoeing ass. You keep on fucking with these bitches you done met at the club! One day you gone wake up and that lil nigga you call a dick gone be lying beside you, because it done fell the fuck off. Anyway, your brother had a rough day, and he needs his rest. When he gets up and is ready to eat, he will be here. Until then shut the fuck up and eat your food!" Ma fussed, and I was bent the fuck over in laughter.

One thing about our parents, they didn't give a damn what came out of their mouths. Nor did they care about how they talked to us. We were all cool like that, but my pops didn't play that shit about his wife. He would fuck us up if we went back and forth with Ma. We may seem like a dysfunctional family, but we were close, and when one of us were in trouble, you could bet we were all coming, guns blazing. About thirty minutes later, Mega walked into the kitchen, and he didn't look happy.

"Hey, baby. How you feeling?" Ma looked over at him, waiting on him to respond.

"I'm good. I know I will have to pay her bills until she goes back to work, but I didn't tell her ass that. I haven't even called her back since I hung up on her. Her mouth is too much for a nigga like me. Maybe after I get some food in me and a drink, I will be in a better mood," Mega said to Ma, and Meech and I was sitting here confused as hell.

"Bro, you in trouble?" I had to ask, because if he needed me, I was ready to ride.

"Nah, I'm good. Some chick walked out in front my car this morning." He said he was good, but I knew he was pissed about that shit.

"How is our business going?" Pops asked, looking over at Mega.

"The numbers are good, so far we've doubled what we brought in last month." Mega smiled, knowing that Pop wouldn't show any emotion.

"Good." Is all he had to say and went back to eating his dinner. Mega chuckled and looked over at Meech and I. Pop and Mega always bumped heads over the business. Even though he stepped away from the game, he still thinks Mega is supposed to run shit the way he did it. I was with my brother on that shit. Pop was stuck back in the eighties and nineties era. It's 2020, times have changed, and Mega was doing this shit with his eyes closed. We were seeing numbers that this empire has never seen before. So, Pop need to chill the fuck out and go rub on Ma booty or something.

"I need to talk to you two. After dinner, we need to go back to Meech crib for a meeting." This nigga Mega done lost his damn mind. I'm not going to that nigga house. They can meet with my ass outside. Fuck that. What the fuck I look like sitting on the couch, and that bitch ass non-human tiger walk in and sit next to me chilling like her ass really belong there? Like that shit ain't even the fuck normal.

"Nah, nigga, I'm not going over to this nigga house. We can talk right the fuck here where it's safe with my muthafuckin' mama, her three eighty, and my fuckin' nine!" I mugged his ass. Mega knew damn well I wasn't about to take my ass nowhere near Meech crib.

"Nigga, Lana ain't thinking bout yo ass! Talia was just over there, and she didn't fuck with her." Meech shrugged his shoulder and smirked.

"That's because that lil bitch knew my three eighty was gone win that war. I don't know why you got that lil hoe, knowing my baby scared of her. Your brother should come first, but I'm gone give you fair warning. If that shit turns on you, and fuck with Mega, or Marco, I'mma kill that hoe! Then I'm gone finish fucking yo ass up." Meech waved her off, as Ma continued to talk her shit.

"Fuck it! I got to handle some shit anyway, but tomorrow we will meet up at the club," Mega spoke as he stood to leave. I needed to get home; I haven't heard from Drieka ass all damn day. She was always doing some shit that made me want to beat the shit out her. My mama didn't raise us to be hitting on no damn woman. Talia always told us that we couldn't hit no girl, but she would beat a bitch down for us if needed. Until this day, those rules still applied. Ma couldn't stand Drieka's ass. She has been waiting for the day to come and beat the shit out of my girl.

Drieka and I have been together for four years, and at first, I thought she was the one for me, but after we got together and made shit official, her true colors came out. All she did was party, get high, and spend my damn money. Drieka was a dark-skinned beauty, she didn't have a big ass, and tits like my brothers were into, but she was just right for me, and I swear I loved that girl. Lately, she's been moving funny. Coming home all times of night, jumping when her phone rings, and going into another room to talk on her phone. One thing I do know. If I find out that she's cheating, I'm killing her, and that bitch nigga she fuckin' with.

"I'm out, I will catch y'all tomorrow." I dapped my brothers up and gave my mother a hug. My pop left the table after he finished eating. I didn't even go say bye to his ass. I will just catch him later. When I made it home, I could hear Drieka on the phone talking.

"Babe, you know I miss you. I will make sure we get together tomorrow," this bitch said to whoever she was fuckin' talking to. I bust right in the room on a fuckin' thousand.

"Who the fuck you talkin' to?" I mugged this bitch, and she looked as if she was going to shit on herself. She threw the phone on the bed and jumped up, walking towards me. If she knew what was best for her, she wouldn't get in my damn face.

"Baby, I was talking to Steph. Why are you coming in here yelling at me like that?" She questioned me, with tears in her eyes as she grabbed my arm. I used to hate to see my woman cry, but right now her tears weren't doing shit but pissing me the fuck off.

"Get the fuck off of me!" I roared, as my chest heaved in and out. I moved quickly to the bed and grabbed her cell phone. She rushed over, and this bitch literally tried to snatch the shit out of my hand. I pushed her back and opened her phone, scrolling to the last person she spoke with, and the shit said Steph.

"I told you it was Steph!" She yelled, trying to grab her phone. I hit the call button and placed it on speaker. I was sent to voicemail. I tried calling the number again, and I got the same thing. I threw her phone on the bed.

"If you think for one second that I won't find out, you're sadly mistaken. Just know that when I do know for certain, it's a wrap for yo ass!" I gritted in her face, walked off into the bathroom, and locked the door. I may play around with my brothers, but I don't play that disrespect shit. Especially not from my damn woman.

MEGA...

"What?" I yelled into the phone. It was the damn girl I hit, and she was blowing my phone up. What if a nigga had to come up on the money, and she was rushing me and shit? Lil mama was stressing me out and I didn't even know her name.

"Don't yell at me when you the one that offered to give me the money. I'm telling yo ass how much it cost me, and I need to know when you plan on giving it." Lil mama was pressed, and I just wanted her to get the fuck on. Walking over to the safe on my wall, I put in my code and then placed my hand on it. Once it opened, I started grabbing stacks out of it.

"Learn how to talk to a nigga, and you won't be put on hold. I don't do the smart mouth shit, so fix yo tone if you want something from me. Were you just visiting, or do you stay in the building?" I could hear her sigh, but I didn't give a fuck about all that. I knew I should have been bought me a house, but my condo worked just fine up until now.

"I live on three."

"Aight, I'm in the penthouse, come get this bread." When she went silent instead of saying okay, I knew it was about to be another problem.

"My leg is broken, how the fuck am I gone come get it." Pinching the bridge of my nose, I stopped myself from telling her ass she wasn't getting shit. Knowing this would get her out of my life, I decided to take it to her. Grabbing five racks, I closed my safe.

"What's the number, man?"

"I'm in 3121." She hung up and I decided to make her wait. Going in the kitchen, I poured me a drink cause I knew I was going to need the shit dealing with her ass. Thirty minutes later, I walked to the elevator and went down. When I got to her door, it showed me how much I didn't know about decorating and shit. Her ass had plants and welcome mats sitting outside her shit. It was also shoes on the mat, letting me know she wanted mufuckas to take their shoes off. Ignoring that, I knocked on the door. Lil mama swung it open looking mad as fuck.

"You said you were on your way down. I stood at this fucking door for five minutes waiting on yo ass. That shit was inconsiderate. Do you know how hard it is to stand on one damn leg?" Looking down, I laughed at her trying to hold her balance.

"Looks like you getting the hang of that shit. Look out." When I tried to walk in, she threw her hand up to stop me, but I pushed past her ass. I was a nosy nigga, and I wanted to make sure lil mama wasn't lying to me. Plus, I wanted to see what other shit she had done to her place, so I could steal some ideas. My shit was bland as hell.

"You can't just walk in my shit and you need to remove your shoes." Sitting down on her white couch, I crossed my feet at the ankles.

"My shit cost more than yo carpet, fuck out of here. This a nice spot. It don't look like you need my bread at all." When she started hopping towards me, I laughed under my breath. I could have helped her, but fuck her and that bum ass leg. If she didn't have such a smart mouth, I would have tried to carry her over.

"Can you just give me the money so I can get back in bed, please?" Grabbing the money, I reached it out to her and then pulled it back when she tried to get it.

"How much you say you needed again?" This time she did roll her eyes.

"It was thirteen hundred and I can't go to work. So, I'm going to need more than that. Normally, I don't ask people for shit, but it is yo fault I'm in this predicament." Was this her way of asking me nicely?

"Let's get this straight; I don't have to give you shit. I'm being nice cuz I feel bad for yo limp legged ass, but don't try and play me, lil mama. You will lose. Here is five racks, that should be enough." When I stood up and threw the money at her, she burst into tears, and that stopped me in my tracks. "Fuck wrong with you?" I said while gritting.

"Even though you're acting like an ass, I appreciate it. I had no idea if you were going to keep your word, especially since that was a week ago, but thank you. I'll figure the rest out, but this is greatly appreciated." Looking around her place, I could see how that probably wasn't enough. Lil mama had expensive taste. You could tell from the way her shit looked.

"I didn't say that was all I was giving you. Well, I did say that, but I'mma help you. Stop that crying shit though, cuz I don't like feeling like a soft nigga. We'll figure something out. Can you cook?" She looked at me like I was crazy. I wasn't asking the mufucka to cook for me, I was trying to see if she could do shit for herself.

"How Sway?"

"Who the fuck is Sway? My name Mega; don't get gripped up." When she laughed, I knew it was something I was missing.

"It doesn't matter and I'm Brielle. No, I can't stand long enough to cook," she said with a smile on her face.

"Aight, I'll have my girl cook you up something and bring it over." When she scrunched her face up, that shit pissed me off. "Ion know what the fuck you looking like that for. I don't have to have her cooking you shit," I yelled while mugging her.

"I'll manage. I don't need yo girlfriend spitting in my shit because she thinks something is going on." Realizing what she assumed when I said girl, I calmed down.

"My girl is my mama. Simmer down, Crip." Not waiting for her to respond, I headed out. I was starting to feel like I belonged in that bitch, and I ain't want to send lil mama mixed signals. Soon as I got back in my spot, I hit up my mama.

"Yeah, son. How you feeling?" She asked, concerned.

"Brielle started crying on me and shit. Talking about nobody ever did shit nice for her. She up there fucked up, so I told her you would bring her some food over to cook. Is that cool?" The line went quiet, so I thought she didn't hear me. "Ma, can you bring her some food."

"Nigga, I heard you the first fucking time. I don't know why you volunteering me and shit. My name ain't Florence and the hoe ain't moving on up. You better go buy her something, hell I look like?" I wasn't sure if it was a rhetorical question or if she was really asking.

"You said you wanted to help. This is the help I'm asking for. If I was that weak ass nigga Marco asking, you would have no problems doing the shit."

"You better watch yo fucking mouth before I come over there and shoot you in yo shit," my pops warned. I don't even know how the nigga heard me. Fuck was he doing listening in on the call and shit?

"Ma, you coming or what?"

"Don't rush me, I'll be over there. Hope the bitch choke on one of these bones. She prolly lying anyway. I've told a few in my days. Maine, I'll only be a few. Be naked when I get back. I'mma put this thang on you."

"What the fuck? Ion wanna hear that shit. In there telling that grown ass man to lay across the bed naked and shit." Not even responding, she hung up. I knew that meant she was gone slap my ass on sight, but I was dead ass. They had no filter and that shit was nasty as fuck. Nobody wanted to hear that.

Knowing my mama was on the way, I started grabbing shit cleaning up. If she came in my shit and it was dirty, she wouldn't shut the fuck up, and I wasn't in the mood for her mouth. I needed to think about what I was going to do about Brielle, and I wasn't for my mama shit. Wiping off the counters, I put up the towels. As soon as I got done making sure it was straight, she was walking inside.

"You better had cleaned this shit up. I can still smell the Pine sol in this bitch. I just don't understand how I got some nasty ass, disrespectful, dumb ass kids. Take me to this bitch house. She better be worth my stew or I'mma fuck you up." Her ass was yelling like we weren't standing in the same room.

"For once, can you quit talking shit? I had enough of that shit for one day." Her ass didn't even respond, just walked out the door. Following behind her, I hit the button on the elevator. Soon as we went downstairs and knocked, it dawned on me that this might not have been a good idea. What if lil mama had a nigga? I didn't even grab my piece.

"Ma, you strapped?"

"Like baby boots and Velcro loops." I didn't even bother to ask what the fuck she was talking about. All that mattered was she had her gun on her. Brielle opened the door and she looked wore the fuck out. I could tell she was tired of hopping around on that leg and shit.

"Oh, you pretty. Not like them stripper bitches with the bullet holes he normally bring home. I don't mind cooking for you. Move out the way jangaleg, I need to put this shit down. Standing there with yo mouth open and shit like you slow. Are you slow, baby? It don't matter, Mega shallow anyway. As long as you got a big ass, everything else is kind of extra. This a nice place, do you sell ass?" I was so embarrassed.

"Umm, no ma'am," she said nervously.

"No, what?" This lady actually leaned forward like she was waiting on an answer. Shaking my head, I sat down. This was about to be a mess.

Brielle...

I'm glad this rude ass nigga finally showed up. When he hung up on me, I didn't think he was going to take care of my bills. I was so damn pissed; I couldn't do shit but cry. I had money saved up, but most of my money went to paying my bills and paying for my classes. I was in Law school at Drexel University. I got some scholarships and student loans, but even with all of that, it still wasn't enough for me to attend school.

I had no one to help me like that. My brother Shawn, and my sister Dream had their own shit to take care of. It was bad enough that we all had to pitch in and make sure our mama, Lola, was straight. Our mama was on drugs and alcohol so bad that she didn't really care about shit else. We helped her by making sure her bills for her apartment was paid, and she had food to eat. We damn sure learned our lesson by giving her the money. None of that shit was used for her bills. The lights were turned the hell off, and we had to come up with the money that we really didn't have fuckin' with her. From that moment on, we didn't give her shit, we paid the shit ourselves. I be damned if she was gone use the money I made to feed her fucking addiction.

"Yo, lil mama, did you hear me?" His question jolted me from my thoughts.

"No, I didn't. What did you say?" I looked over at him, waiting for him to repeat his question. Damn, this man was fine; everything about his ass was perfect. He was tall, deep brown eyes, suckable fucking lips, and he was cut up in all the right places. His dreads were so neat, and his beard was nicely trimmed.

"Damn, I'm gone stop talking to your ass. Every time I ask you something, you zone the fuck out." He mugged me, and I was so damn embarrassed.

"I'm sorry, I'm just not used to having company. The only person that comes to visit me is my sister, and brother and that's not often." I smiled at him, just as my doorbell went off. I tried to get up, but with the condition I was in, it was a damn struggle.

"I got it." Mega jumped up to answer my door. His mama sure had it smelling good in here. I wondered what she was cooking. I hated to tell them that I was a picky eater. The way she came in, let me know that she would curse my ass out. Mega came walking in the room with a bouquet of beautiful roses.

"I guess your nigga was letting you know he was thinking about you," he spoke with an attitude, as he mugged me.

"Ummm, I'm not sure who these are from......" I was cut off by him calling out for his mama.

"Ma, let's go! She can handle the rest," he yelled out, and I was sitting here looking at him crazy. Like, I know this nigga don't have no damn attitude over flowers. I don't even know who sent the fucking flowers, but why the fuck would he get mad? We don't even know each other like that, and he damn sure isn't my man.

"Ma!" He yelled out again to his mother.

"Nigga, why the fuck you keep yelling my damn name! I'm in here trying to fix this cripple ass girl some damn food, that you called me over here to do. Curly Sue, what the fuck you did to my damn son?" She questioned, looking in my direction.

"Ummm... I didn't do anything. He answered the door and got pissed because someone sent me flowers," I nervously spoke, because right now, I felt like I was ten years old.

"Nigga, I know damn well you ain't sitting yo big goofy, dumb ass in here mad because some nigga done sent her flowers? How the fuck you gone get mad over some shit like... Ahhhhhh hell nawl! Already? You're feeling her ass already? You just met the damn heifer!" She fussed and walked back in the kitchen.

"I'm not feeling shit, just hurry up," he snapped, he sat down in the chair, mugging the hell out of me. I couldn't believe that he was this mad over some shit that he knew nothing about. Hell, I don't even have a man. I lifted the card from the flowers to see who sent them.

'I'm thinking about you, baby. Love L' Is what the card read. *Fuckkkk! How the fuck did he know where I was staying? I thought to myself.*

The flowers were from my ex Lenox. His ass is the real reason I got hit by Mega. I was on the phone arguing with his dumb ass, and not paying attention to where the fuck I was going. I left Lenox about six months ago, cause that nigga was a piece of shit. I went through so much shit with him the three years that we were together. He was putting his hands on me, talking to me all disrespectful and cheating on me. For years I was afraid to leave his ass, because he always said that he would kill me if I did.

One night we were at his brother's house for a family gathering, this chick Sabrina was there. Her family was close to Lenox's family, so I really didn't think anything of it. I hadn't been to any of the family functions in a while. She was pregnant, and I asked her how far along she was, and she said she was five months. Then the bitch had the nerve to have a smirk on her face, watching everything I did with Lenox. About an hour or so into the dinner, she walked up to me and told me that her and Lenox were seeing each other for the past year and that her baby was his. I spazzed on her ass and then confronted him. This bitch ass nigga acted as if he did nothing wrong. Talking bout I'm his girl, and she just the bitch that's having his baby, but we were going to raise the baby together, the three of us.

Like what the fuck was that nigga smoking? I cursed his ass out, and he beat the shit out of me, while everyone watched. Nobody said nothing. When I got myself together, I left and went home. I packed as much shit as I could and left his ass. Now he's threatening me one minute and then sending gifts the next, trying to get me to come back. Fuck that nigga! Mega talking on his phone interrupted my thoughts. When I looked at him, he was talking but still staring me down.

"Alright, I'm done. I made you some stewed chicken breast with gravy, and potatoes. That should hold you over for a couple of days. Do you have family that can help you?" His mother questioned, as she sat beside me on the couch.

"No, ma'am, but I think I can handle it from here. I don't want to bother you. I appreciate you both for helping me." I smiled, because I truly did appreciate their kindness. I didn't expect any of this from him, other than to pay my medical bills.

"Nah, we not gone leave you hangin'. Besides, Mega gone pay me for my damn services. I will stop by and check on you in a couple of days. What's your name? I hate to call you bitch; I will save that for them cum bucket hoes they decide to bring home. You seem like a nice girl, and respectful too." She laughed, as she pulled her phone out of her purse.

"Ohh, my name is Brielle." It's bad that she's been in my kitchen cooking, and we didn't know each other's names.

"I'm Talia, put your number in my phone, so that I can call you before I just pop up on you. I hate when niggas do that shit. Like mufucka call before you just come over to my shit. My man might have me in the air, hittin' it sideways and shit. I have to tell my sons all the time about that shit. One day they ass gone see some shit they ain't ready for. Me and my nigga always trying some new shit out." She laughed, and I did too. She was funny as hell, and I think I was going to like Mrs. Talia.

"Ma, I don't want to hear that shit. Ain't yo ass finished cooking?" Mega had his face all twisted, looking at his mama.

"Nigga, don't be no damn hater cause you can't do what yo daddy can! The fuck wrong with you? You just all in your feelings because Bri here got a nigga sending her flowers, with yo mad ass." She laughed, as she said goodbye to me and walked out. I thought he was going to leave with her, but he was still here.

"Thank you for all of this." I wanted to say more, but the stare down he was giving me made me a little uncomfortable.

"You sure you're going to be alright?" He questioned, as he stood there.

"I'm just going to get back in bed; there isn't much I can do." Which was true, I could barely use the damn crutches I was on. He walked over, lifting me into his arms, and I could have melted right there. Without thinking, I laid my head on his muscular chest. Once I told him where my bedroom was, he walked in and laid me in the bed. What confused the fuck out of me, is when he took off his shoes and laid in the damn bed next to me.

"Excuse me, what are you doing?" I had to question him, because he damn sure wasn't getting no ass from me.

"I'm being nice, now turn the damn television on and be happy that I'm here with your ass," he snapped as he got comfortable, leaving my ass looking at him sideways. I never said if I had a man to him directly. *What the fuck if I did have one?* It seems that he really didn't give a damn if I did or not!

MEECH...

Looking around the room, I was ready to get the fuck on about my day. All my brothers were with a hoe, and I was sitting here next to Talia ass listening to her smacking and shit on this chicken bone. Her food was fye, but she ain't have to be eating the shit like that. Seeing Mega jump up and running to get this girl he was with another plate had me sick to my stomach. He only been hanging around this girl for a week, and his ass was acting sprung and shit. I'm still confused on why he even brought her here.

"Damn, shorty hemmed you up for some money, and now you catering to her? You gotta do better, bro. She got you out here looking like a goofy." Talia slapped me across my lip with her gnawed on chicken bone.

"Don't do that." Ignoring her, I continued gritting at Mega.

"Calm down with yo angry ass. I fucked her up, so I'm helping her out. You know, that's what decent people do." Mega said that shit like he was begging me to stop. He knew that shit wasn't my style, so I kept going.

"I'm saying though, didn't you give her a bunch of bread? Then why the fuck you out here acting like yo name Geoffrey and shit. Canyons to the left of them, canyons to the right of them face ass." Talia slow ass threw her hands in the air like Geoffrey did on Fresh Prince, and we fell out laughing.

"I can leave if it's a problem. You know I don't want to start any trouble." The girl he was with was trying to look innocent and shit.

"How you gone leave? My brother gone have to carry yo limp ass out of here, right? Then shut the fuck up." Talia slapped me on the leg again.

"Don't take offense, girl. They been treating me like that for years. It's how they are." Marco's girl, Drieka was trying to joke, but she knew not to play that shit with me.

"That's cuz we don't like yo big foot ass. Just sit there and shut yo ass up, goat neck ass mufucka."

"Baaaaa baaaaa." Talia started making goat sounds, and we started laughing again.

"Bro, I been trying to figure out what kind of neck she had, but the shit wasn't coming to me. A lil old ass Billy goat gruff." Mega shook his head as he laughed, but the girl with him gave him a look telling him to stop.

"You never defend me against them. Your brothers have no respect for me," Drieka whined like a lil ass kid.

"That's because he can't run and tell his mama on us, cuz she don't like yo ass either. Ion know what you thought he was gone do anyway, besides get beat the fuck up."

"Guess I need to go put the lamb chops back in the fridge. I'm sure she don't want to eat her kin. Come on, Billy. Help me put Cousin Pete back in the freezer." Talia got up, and I fell out laughing. I swear we hated that bitch Drieka, and that's because she cheated on baby bro when they first got together. His ass was sprung and refused to leave her. Everyone knew she was after his money, but him. I would never fuck with that hoe.

Talia came back out, sat on pop's lap, and I looked around at everyone again. Over this lovey-dovey shit, I stood up and dropped my trash and plate on Drieka's lap. The way she gasped had me laughing hard as hell. Marco looked towards Talia for help, but she high-fived me and laughed. Drieka looked as if she was about to say something she was so pissed.

"Don't get yo lil feelings hurt. Trash bitches get trashed; accept it, and move on. Son, where you going?" Talia shut her ass down quick.

"I'm not with all this relationship shit. You know me, I'm on the way to find me a big booty stripper, and you know the rest." Not waiting on a response, I walked out and jumped on my bike. Zipping my jacket up, I threw my helmet on and took off. It was cold out tonight, but I loved being in the breeze. A nigga loved being free in all aspects of my life. Pulling into the strip club, I went inside and sat at my regular table. It was some loud mouth chick at the next table screaming at the strippers like she had a dick on swoll. This stripper named Dusse walked over to me and instantly started dancing on me.

"Hey, daddy. You haven't been in here in a while. You don't miss this ass?" Licking my lips, I gripped her ass and let her bounce on my shit. The waitress brought over my usual bottle and walked off.

"It's only been a week, but you know I will always come back to this ass. Do that thing I like." Smiling, she did a handstand and started twerking in the air. The loud mouth next to me started yelling out annoying ass shit.

"Damn, if you put that much effort into a job, yo ass would be ugly paid." Ignoring her, I continued to throw all my money on Dusse. By this time, my dick was hard as hell, and I was ready to fuck.

"Daddy, I see you ready to go in the back room or is this one of the nights you want me at yo crib so we can go all night?" Thinking it over, I wanted to relieve some stress.

"We can head to my spot." Standing up, I got ready to head out when loud mouth started talking shit.

"Oh, you one of them type of niggas. Can't get a real woman or cheating on yo bitch with some nasty ass stripper. Get the fuck out of here." Turning to her, I walked over and stood over her loud ass.

"Who the fuck you talking to, yo? Do you know who the fuck I am?" She started laughing hard as hell, and it kind of pissed me off. I don't know who she is, but she was about to find out who the fuck I was soon.

"I don't give a fuck who you are, lil nasty ass nigga. Fuck out of my face." Before I could say anything, Dusse stepped up.

"Bitch, I'mma ask you nicely to get the fuck up out of my club before I drag yo hostile ass up out of here." The look loud mouth gave when she stood up had me wondering which one of they ass had me turned on more.

"Drag me? Show me you that tough, ol' helmet head ass bitch." Before Dusse could show her, loud mouth swung on her and went crazy. I've never seen someone so little fight that hard. Lil mama was going crazy, and I couldn't do shit but laugh. Security finally came over and tried to drag loud mouth out of the club. Her ass was fighting like a nigga was trying to take her booty hole. Stepping in, I grabbed her and pulled her close to me.

"Hey, I got her. She good. Lil mama, calm yo ass down. If you hit me, I'mma knock yo ass out." Since she was so close, I could tell she was drunk as hell.

"You ain't gone do shit." Knowing she couldn't stay in the club; I took her outside. As soon as we got out the door, I dropped her ass. "What the fuck?!" Loudmouth looked around trying to figure out what was going on.

"You might don't know who I am, but you gone respect me like you do. Now, get yo drunk ass up and go home."

"You take me; I didn't drive. Just know yo nasty ass ain't getting no pussy. You fuck stripper bitches." Laughing, I leaned down as if I was going to help her up.

"Walk on yo lips, big mouth ass mufucka." Without giving her time to respond, I walked off and left her ass looking dumb. Jumping on my bike, I rode off, looking for some pussy.

DREAM...

Rolling over, I looked at Brielle, staring at me in disgust. My head was pounding, and I felt like shit. Normally, I don't drink like that, but I had a rough ass day yesterday. Shit was all bad and I needed a turn up. Lola needed help with a bill and I really ain't have it like that to give, but Bri couldn't give it to her since she hadn't been at work. I hadn't been able to reach my brother, so I had to bite the fucking bullet and give it to her. Working at Aldi's paid a nice lil amount, but not enough for me to be taking care of a grown mufucka that don't wanna stop getting high.

Right after I left Lola's, I go to my nigga Hill's crib, only to find him fucking a stripper. It was how I ended up at the club drinking, ready to fight all them bitches. Yeah, I fucked Hill and that bitch up, but I wanted to whoop all them hoes off GP. I didn't expect to be dropped on my ass and left in the parking lot like a Mc Donald's bag. I had no choice but to hit up an Uber to come and get me. As drunk as I was, I prayed

my driver didn't try to kidnap and rape me.

"Bitch, get the fuck up. It's three in the afternoon and I

got company coming over." She was yelling and I didn't want

to hear it. My head was splitting in half, or at least that's what

it felt like.

"Stop yelling. If you had the day I did yesterday, you

would be right here looking like Eddie Kang Jr. right with me.

Can a bitch get some juice and an aspirin?" Bri rolled her eyes

and didn't move. I knew her leg was broken, but I still wanted

her to help me. Hell, she was getting around pretty good, hip-

hopping on that bitch.

"Naw, you can get up and go get it yourself though. I

don't care what happened, there is no reason for you to get

this drunk. Your ass talked shit all night, but I had no idea

what the hell you was talking about." Not responding to her, I

got up and took a minute-long piss. Soon as I was done, I

looked in her medicine cabinet and grabbed some aspirin.

The bougie bitch had glasses in her bathroom, so I grabbed one and drunk some water to wash down the pill. Walking back in the room and sitting on the bed, I tried to explain to her what happened.

"Yo mama will have anybody drunk, first of all, but she not the only reason. I'm done with Hill's ass. Caught that nigga fucking a stripper and I beat his ass."

"Bitch, a strippperrr? How you know she was a stripper?" Bri asked all in it with her mouth open.

"cause me and that nigga done been in there a few times. Bitch used to be my favorite, but fuck her. I beat her ass too."

"I told you about being nasty. You ain't have no business hanging out in a strip club anyway. That's like opening Pandora's box. If you went there to fight, you must have gotten yo ass beat. Your ass was laid out in here like a nigga in a casket." Throwing a pillow at her, I rolled my eyes and continued with my story.

"Naw, bitch. I saw some nigga in there about to leave and go fuck a stripper, and I snapped. Beat the bitch up, got put out the club, then he dropped me on my ass because of my mouth. Nigga left me there with his ugly ass. I'm just tired." She looked shocked.

"So, you got treated by an ugly nigga?" Bri asked, confused.

"Naw, sis. He was fine as hell. Nigga body was built from the Gods, and his teeth was perfect. I felt a way though, cause his hair longer than mine. His dreads was down his back, but I swear in another day and time, I would have climbed that tree. Whew. Anyway, fuck niggas. I'm about to find me a bitch that likes eating pussy but don't want to touch or kiss me." She looked at me crazy and we both fell out laughing.

"With your luck, you gone end up with a big, burly bitch named Fontaine." Crying tears, I doubled over from laughing so hard. She wasn't lying. Hearing her doorbell sound off, I gave her a menacing look and got up to go answer the door. It was a fine ass nigga standing there with food in his hand.

"Well damn. You so fine you can run me over." Bri came from the back hopping on one leg, and I looked at her strangely. She was just limping on the other one. She could barely walk on it, but she wasn't hopping around like this.

"Hey, Mega. Come in. Ooh, what is that? It smells good." This bitch was breathing hard and acting like she could barely make it. His ass scooped her up and carried her to the couch. I stood there watching in disbelief.

"Ummm, well hello. I'm her sister Dream. What you bring us to eat?" Bri shot me a look that said get the fuck out.

"Nice to meet you and it's Chinese. Brielle, you want a lil bit of everything or just beef fried rice?" This nigga blew me off as if I wasn't standing there talking to his ass.

"Damn, can I have some too or am I just invisible in this bitch?"

"Sis, I told you I had plans. I'll make it up to you when my leg feels better. You can gone and head out now." Laughing sarcastically, I scoffed at this fake ass hoe. I wasn't really mad, but I damn sure was about to be petty.

"Your leg felt better a while ago when you was walking around this bitch. Now you in here acting handicapped and gone put me out, so you can eat rat and fake with this nigga? You ain't shit. I'll leave though since he's fine as hell. You better suck something since you want me to go." Her eyes damn near popped out of her head. She threw one of those hard ass fancy pillows at me, and I laughed and went to the room to get my stuff.

Realizing I didn't drive, I pulled out my phone and requested an Uber. Throwing on my shoes, I grabbed my shit and went downstairs to wait. Out of nowhere, a bike pulled up, and I damn near choked on my spit. It was the guy from last night and he looked even better in the daylight. His ass swerved my way, and I had to jump back to keep from getting hit.

"Muthafucka! You are one ignorant ass nigga. Fuck are you doing?" His ass parked and got off. Not saying a word, he snatched me up like he was about to beat my ass.

"What the fuck did I tell you last night, yo? Watch yo fucking mouth before I break that bitch." First, I just stared at him, then I laughed.

"You do realize you don't scare me, right? I'mma need you to dress the part if you want to be a big scary ass nigga." Letting me down, he looked at me like he didn't know what I meant.

"You don't have to be scared to get fucked up, and what the fuck are you talking about?" His ass damn near spit on me he was talking so rough.

"I'm just saying, how you tough and you got on them tight ass pants. Hell, how you riding a bike in them bitches? Yo nuts gots to be on swoll in them mufuckas. Don't look at me like that. I'm just saying the shit gotta hurt." His anger went away and he fell out laughing. I was expecting him to throw out more threats. Instead, he licked his lips, and my pussy jumped.

"So, what you saying is you want to eat dis dick? I get it. You have to try and use jokes as a defense mechanism. Don't worry, this bitch big, so you'll love it. When you wanna hook up?" Scoffing, I shook my head at his ass.

"You are full of yo self, my nigga. I don't eat dick and I don't suck chafed balls." His sexy ass laughed again.

"Yeah, you wanna lick these mufuckas. How bout I give you my number and you hit me up later? You owe me anyway after fucking up my pussy last night. Yeah, that shit gone be fye. I've never had good faith head before." His ass reached in my hand and snatched my phone. The Uber driver pulled up and I asked him to wait.

"Nigga, give me my phone; he waiting on me." The smile again.

"I'm Meech, but it won't matter after tonight. I never fuck the same mufucka twice. I'll make sure the shit is mind-blowing though. You can't be mad about that shit." His arrogant ass really just said that shit. I couldn't believe his ass was this cocky. Fine, but cocky.

"I won't be calling you. I'm good. You seem to have your own balls in your hands. Jack them bitches, mmk." Snatching my phone back, I walked towards the car.

"Are you going to at least tell me your name, loudmouth?" Now it was my turn to laugh.

"It's Dream. You know, like the wet dream you are going to have tonight." His ass walked towards the door and looked back.

"You too worried about my balls when you should be trying to figure out why your grown ass don't have a car. You in strip clubs and shit, but no whip. Fix yo life bruh. My dick change lives. It's straight." His ass went inside leaving me standing there wanting to beat his ass. Getting in the Uber, I leaned my head back and waited on him to take me to my car.

I swear I hate niggas.

MARCO...

Drieka and I were on our way home from my parent's house full as hell. Ma made my favorite fried chicken, mac & cheese, and some greens, and I wanted some more of that shit. I was still pissed about how Meech and my mom treated her at dinner the other night. Ma was fucking with her again tonight, but I thanked God Meech ass wasn't there. It was true when Drieka and I first got together she cheated on me, and it wasn't that I was weak.

I did my best to forgive and work shit out with her. When I forgave her, I told her then that I wasn't going for that shit ever again. She knew if it did happen again, we were done, and I might kill her ass this time. With me, that shit will depend on which way the wind is blowing that day. Meech hated her ass the most. He was with me the night I found out she cheated on me.

When I let it ride, my brother cursed me out and didn't speak to me for a couple of weeks. I don't have the same mentality as him; he doesn't give a damn about a woman's feelings. Meech is that way because he got hurt by his ex, Tasha. He was in love with her ass, but she got pregnant by another dude and left him. Ever since then that nigga has been a rude asshole when it comes to women and relationships. He wanted me to be the same, but I wasn't built like that.

"Why you let them talk to me like that? I'm sick of their asses. Normally you would defend me, but you just let them go, and that shit isn't cool!" She continued to argue, as we walked in the house. I let them do them because I was still pissed about that call she was on the other night.

"Driek, you always going back and forth with them, and the other night was no fuckin' different. Besides, I'm surprised you had time to even notice that they were fucking with you. You were so deep in your phone; I didn't think you even cared." She fanned me off, avoiding what I just said to her. She didn't say shit when we came home, but now that Ma was fucking with her, she wanted to bring the shit up.

"I'm going to fix us a drink. I will be right back." She walked out of the room, and I shook my head. I headed in the bathroom to jump in the shower and handle my hygiene. When I was done, Drieka was standing in the bathroom, sipping on her drink as she handed me mine.

"You seem so uptight, drink this and let's enjoy the rest of our night." She smiled and kissed me on the lips. I downed the drink and walked into the bedroom, so I could relax. Drieka went to take a shower, and I turned the television on. That was the last thing that I remembered.

My phone was going off, and I jumped up in the bed, looking around. It was now daylight outside. Damn, I must have fallen asleep last night cause I damn sure don't remember shit. My phone stopped ringing and started back up. I grabbed it and it was Mega calling.

"Yeah," I spoke groggily into the phone.

"Meet me at Meech crib, and I don't want to hear shit about you not coming. Be there in thirty, and why the fuck is you still sleeping? It's damn near two in the afternoon, nigga," this grumpy nigga spoke and hung up. I glanced at Drieka's side of the bed, and that shit was all made up. Shit was strange, but I shook it off and hopped in the shower, so I could go see what the hell my brothers wanted. About an hour later, I was dressed and walking out. I assumed Drieka had some shit to do since she was already gone. I jumped in my car and headed out Springfield to Meech crib. I pulled in the driveway next to Mega's car, hoping he had Lana ass put the fuck up. I swear if that bitch come near me, I'm shooting her ass. When I walked in the house, I heard them talking in the living room.

"Damn, nigga, I spoke to yo ass over an hour ago." Mega's face was twisted the fuck up as he spoke.

"I had to get dressed. What the fuck was I supposed to do walk around with smelly ass balls? What the fuck y'all got going on?" I questioned, as I plopped down in the chair.

"Nigga, you break my shit, you gone pay for that shit!" This nigga Meech was talking out the side of his neck.

"Man, fuck this cheap ass furniture!" I yelled, fucking with his sensitive ass.

"Can y'all shut the fuck up! I got a call from Lenox. He said he needs a reup for two million worth of product. I don't know if I want to give this nigga that much weight. For one, he just copped off our ass about a week ago. Second, I don't really trust that nigga," Mega said nonchalantly as he looked down at his phone.

"We ain't never had no problems from the nigga. I say give him that shit. Money is money in my eyes, and if he trying to reup, let the nigga reup." Meech was always about the money.

"Nigga, money is the bottom line, but when you in the fucking streets you have to be a thinker, a damn planner. The nigga just got bricks from us. Some shit don't feel right about it and I think we gone decline his offer," Mega spoke up, and I agreed with what he was saying.

"I agree with Mega. Even though we don't have an issue with him, he may be up to something. I think we should proceed with caution with his ass," I voiced my opinion and Meech face started balling up.

"Nigga, you always agreeing with Mega!" Meech threw out there as he looked over at Mega and smiled. Mega smiled back, and I was looking at these two niggas wondering what the fuck they were smiling for.

"What the fuck you two goofy ass niggas smiling at?" I questioned, and Meech put his hand up.

"Don't make no sudden moves." When that nigga said that, I turned in the direction that he was looking in and immediately started screaming. I jumped on his couch, and that crazy bitch Lana was on my ass. I pulled my damn gun out and started shooting; I didn't give a damn who I fuckin hit. Fuck that! Mmmm, mmmmm, I don't fuck with nothing on four damn legs. Ion know what the fuck they thought this was, but they gone be doing a tiger roast on her ass when I was done with her. These niggas were laughing their ass off until them bullets started flying. Meech was yelling at me not to shoot that lil bitch!

"Nigga, what the fuck is wrong with you?! You could have killed her!" Meech was screaming like it was really his child.

"Fuck that! That bitch could have killed me. This is why I don't come over to your fuckin' house! Y'all always wanna fuck with me, but you keep fucking with me, I'mma put that ugly bitch on a grill somewhere! Y'all play too damn much. I'm bout to call mama on yo ass. You not even supposed to have that hoe, I'm reporting y'all ass to them National wildlife mufukas!" I'm gone pay they ass back for that shit. Mega was still laughing, but I ain't see where the shit was funny.

"You need to loosen the fuck up, go home and get you some pussy, nigga! I saw yo hoe ass woman at the gas station on the Blvd last night. I started to run her ass over." Meech was laughing, but I wasn't.

"You didn't see Drieka, we were together last night, and when we got home, we went to bed."

"Nah, nigga. You went to bed, but I saw yo bitch at the gas station. You act like I don't know what that loose pussy bitch looks like! Nigga I know a loose pussy hoe when I see one, and I saw yo loose pussy hoe last night!" Meech ass was disrespecting her, but I thought about what he said, got up and walked out of his house.

DRIEKA...

I'm so fuckin' sick of Marco and his bitch ass family. All they do is talk shit to me, and I talk shit back. Fuck them. I cheated on him, and ever since that shit went down, they been fuckin' with me. Marco was a fine ass nigga, his muscle toned body was tatted up, and the dick was bomb as fuck, but I couldn't help wanting to fuck other niggas. The nigga I'm fuckin' with now was just as fine as Marco; his dick wasn't as big, but that shit was enough to do some damage.

My new boo wanted me to come out, and I couldn't leave because Marco would have been on my ass. I fixed him a drink and crushed a Percocet up in it. Anytime I needed to get out I would crush some type of drug in his shit. Once he was out, I got up and hauled ass to my man. I knew he wouldn't wake the fuck up until late the next day. So, when his ass got up, he would think I left early, but truth be told my ass was getting dicked the fuck down all night long.

"Bae, I need to get home." I turned over, as he was texting on his phone.

"I thought you were staying with me for the rest of the day." He smiled, pulling me into him as he slid his hand between my legs.

"Ummm, uhhhh, no. I got to go home. I will call you... ohhhh shit!" A loud groan escaped my mouth.

"Mmm, fuck that! Turn that fat ass over," he demanded as he slapped his dick on my ass.

"Fuck!" He slammed his dick inside of me and I screamed out. This shit was so fuckin' good, as he gripped my ass cheeks, pounding the shit out of my pussy. I tried to throw that shit back, but I was losing the battle.

"Stop acting like you don't know how to fuck and take this big mufucka," he growled, and I started moving meeting his thrusts. "Damn, you got some good fuckin' pussy! I'm bout to bust where you want this shit at?" He was digging my back the fuck out.

"Shittt! Cum in me!" I screamed as I started creaming all over his shit.

"You need to leave that nigga. I told you I got you! I'm about to be king in these streets, and I want yo ass beside me when I take over this shit. I might need you to do some shit for me, but I will tell you about it later. I need to put my plan in motion first," Lenox stated, as he slapped me on my ass.

"I got you, bae. Let me work some shit out on my end, and I got you." I kissed his lips and jumped in the shower. My boo was sweet, and I couldn't believe he wanted me by his side. After a round in the shower, I was finally on my way home. I stopped by the mall and ran into Macy's just to buy something to make it seem that I was out shopping. When I walked in the house, Marco was sitting on the couch.

"Where the fuck you been?" The look on his face said that he was pissed the fuck off.

"I been out shopping! Why the fuck you yelling at me?" I looked at him, scrunching my face up.

"Where were you last night?" He calmly asked, and I knew his ass was knocked the fuck out.

"I was home last night, you know that." I nervously smiled.

"Nah, bitch, I don't know that. If you lie to me, I swear I'mma beat yo ass!" He got in my face, and I knew that I needed to come up with some shit quick.

"Okay, okay, bae! I was out with Char; her and Ron were going through some shit, and he hit her. She called me all hysterical and I jumped up to go check on her. I didn't want to wake you, because you were sleeping so good." I was sweating fuckin' bullets. I hope he believed what the fuck I was saying.

"Call her!" This nigga was crazy, and he wasn't gonna stop fuckin' with me until I called Char ass. I pulled my phone out and dialed her number.

"Put that shit on speaker," he spat, and I hit the speaker on my phone.

"Hey, bitch. What's up?" Char sounded like she was out of breath.

"Can you tell Marco what we did last night?" I was praying to GOD that this bitch didn't fuck this up.

"We went out for a drink. Why, what's up?" Char questioned, but I hung up the phone on her ass.

"You heard what she said, and I'm getting tired of you treating me like shit!" I started crying some bullshit ass tears. He walked up to me and pulled me into his arms.

"I'm sorry, Driek. You been moving funny and that shit been fuckin' with me." He lifted my chin and kissed me. He lifted me up, and I knew he wanted some pussy! It was fucked up to fuck him, but he would definitely know

something was up if I didn't. I have never denied him from

getting the pussy. I couldn't afford for us to be in a bad space

right now. I'm gone chill out for a couple of days on Lenox. I

will talk to him and pray to God that his ass would be cool

with it.

"All I'm saying is, you been laid up under this bitch like she yours and shit. Fall back. If you want to help her, do that, but you ain't gotta be catering to her every need." Meech was going off as usual, but I didn't have time to coddle him.

"Look, I told her I will help her out, and that's all I'm doing. She got about four weeks left and then she can get out of my life. Right now, I'm more concerned with this nigga Lenox as you should be as well."

"So, for the next few weeks, you're basically her bitch. I get it. I'm just saying since you like getting fucked, stop bitching about Lenox." I know he didn't like Brielle, but Meech was taking this shit too far.

"Not the same, and I'mma ask you to move the fuck on from it. Dude about to pull up and we need to be focused."

"I wish both of you bitches just shut the fuck up. Meech, you always get like this when you're jealous. You don't like to see mufuckas happy. We get it, you don't like bitches, but we do," Marco said that all wrong, but I laughed because I knew Meech was about to go the fuck off.

"Oh, now I'm the gay one? I'm not the one we caught in the basement with Sammy talking about y'all was playing games. Probably playing pat a ball pat a ball baker's man. Put it in my ass as fast as u ca. Still don't know what happened to this day. All I know is y'all looked guilty than a motherfucker." I laughed because they did, but I also knew it was because he thought it was our mama.

"Nigga, you know I was on punishment, and I thought we got caught." Marco ass always tried to explain the shit, and I had no idea why. He knew damn well we knew his ass wasn't gay, but he let Meech get in his head every time.

"The only thing I know is that Lenox just pulled up. Tuck yo dick and let's have this meeting." Just like that, he dismissed Marco like he wasn't shit. Looking at the look on baby bro face, I couldn't do shit but laugh. As soon as Lenox got out of the car, I wiped that shit off, and we all stepped outside. This nigga walked up with a smug ass look on his face and I wanted to knock that shit right off.

"Aight, let's get down to business. I got two mil with me right now, and I'm trying to get this product. What's up?" Even though Meech always said we should get this money, the look on his face told me he was thinking the same shit as me.

"Slow down, I haven't agreed to anything yet. I need you to tell me why you need this much product, this fast. How do you plan on moving this shit, and where?" This bitch had the nerve to look off like I was getting on his nerves.

"I know you hear a mufucka talking to you. You deaf or some shit? I've never seen a deaf king pin out this bitch." Meech was getting aggravated and so was I.

"Let's just calm down."

"Shut the fuck up," Me and Meech both yelled at Marco. Nigga was always trying to be the peacemaker.

"I didn't know the connect needed to know all this shit. I have the money, and you have the product. We make the fucking trade and go on about our business. What the fuck kind of shit show is this?" Lenox was getting pissed, but it only made me trust him less.

"It's my show, and you still haven't answered my questions. Take some time and think about how you want to answer them and then hit me up. Until then, don't dial my fuckin' number." Without waiting on him to say anything else, I walked off and got in the car. My brothers followed suit.

"I thought we didn't care about shit but the money, what the fuck was that all about?" Marco was throwing questions out there, but that shit was working my nerves.

"You can't be that fucking slow. Nigga all of a sudden wants that much product, but can't tell us why. Some shit ain't right, and until I figure it out, nobody sells him shit. If I find out one brick went his way, y'all gone have to see me."

"You ain't scaring nobody but Marco. You should have had the meeting at my crib. I'm with you, something off about that nigga, and I don't trust it. Should have patted that mufucka down for a wire. Ion think it's smart to even talk around that nigga." Damn, I hadn't even thought about that shit.

"Hey, I'mma drop y'all off. I need to go holla at somebody." Marco looked confused, but Meech nodded.

"Who? We the ones that need to decide on this shit."

"I swear I'm really starting to think you slow as fuck. He going to holla at Pops, dummy. Like damn, I'm starting to think yo bitch ass was adopted. You are the only one with them slick ass cat eyes." They continued to argue all the way to my crib. I didn't even get out of the car, I let them out and drove off.

When I got to my parent's house, Pops was in the back playing golf. I never understood why he got all that land, until I saw him playing. He looked at peace and I guess that's all that mattered. When he saw me coming, he nodded at the clubs and I grabbed one.

"What's wrong? What did you fuck up this time?" This was why I hated coming to him for anything concerning the business.

"Why do you do that? Why do you always assume the fucking worst? If you thought I couldn't do it, then why the fuck you leave the shit to me?" Pops stopped swinging the golf club and mugged me.

"I don't give a fuck how big you think you are. Watch yo fucking tone with me. Don't ever forget who the fuck is really in charge. I asked you a question, and all you need to do is answer it." My jawline clenched as I tried my best not to go off on his ass.

"As much as you would like to think so, I haven't fucked up shit. I needed some advice, but if you're in one of your, 'I'm tired of you being better than me' moods, then I can go."

"Tell me what the fuck you want and leave the attitude on the grass. Swing." Ignoring his tone, I told him why I was there.

"I know you feel like I should just give Lenox the product, but something is telling me the shit ain't right. I asked him what he needed with the product, and his ass couldn't tell me. I don't like him, so I'm trying not to make it personal. I'm just not feeling this nigga." Pops ain't say shit. He just kept hitting the balls for about five minutes.

"In this line of business, you have to learn to trust yo gut. Even when nothing seems out of place, yo gut will always lead you in the right direction. It's how I survived the streets and it's why you have superseded me. Now all you have to do is figure out what to do about the feeling in your gut." Laughing, I looked at him like he was crazy.

"That's why I'm here." His ass shook his head no.

"Naw, bruh. If I was going to do all the work for you, I may as well have stayed in the business. These are things you have to figure out on yo own. Ion got time to babysit you."

"Daddy, come in here and get this puss-... Oh, hey, Mega. I ain't know you was out here. What's going on?" I had nothing to say, so I shook my head and walked off. Getting in my car, I called Bri. I needed to clear my mind, so I decided to go chill out with her. Soon as I hung up, I drove off towards my building. When I pulled in, it looked like Lenox's car leaving out of my parking lot, but I could have been tripping. Even if it was him, nigga couldn't even get on my floor without a passcode. Shaking off the feeling, I parked and headed inside.

BRIELLE...

After hanging up with Mega, I hopped my ass to the bathroom and tried to freshen up. It was hard as hell handling my hygiene with a bum ass leg, but there was no way I was allowing him to come over here, and I'm smelling like freelance pussy. I grabbed my Yoni wash I got from this group on Facebook called Yoni Luv. That shit was life and I lived for it.

After making sure I was as clean as I could be, I brushed my teeth and then hopped back into my room. Sliding on some cute lil boy short pajamas and a tank, I made my way back to the front room, so I could look as if I had been chilling there all day. I've been doing good getting around on my leg, but I played handicap as hell whenever Mega was around. When I first met him, I thought he was mean as hell, but now, whew. Now it took everything in me to control my pussy around him.

He was everything a girl would want in a guy. Strong, fine, sexy, and got it all. Mega made everyone around him feel his strength and I was drawn to it. The entire time I was with Lenox, I felt weak. Less than and he made sure I continued to feel that way. When I was with him, I doubted myself, and my self-esteem was damn near nonexistent. A knock on the door brought me out of my thoughts. If I could, I would have run to the door. Moving as fast as I could, I made it and flung the door open only to have the shock of my life.

"Lenox, what the hell are you doing here?" I'm still confused on how he knew where I lived.

"Fuck wrong with you? Since when is it a crime for me to come see my girl? Are you going to let me in, or do I have to fuck you in the hall?" His ass had a lot of nerve.

"I can't do this. You need to go. Right now!" I kept listening for the elevator to ding, because the last thing I needed was for Mega to show up. When he leaned towards me, I jumped.

"Do what? Be with your man?" His ass was delusional.

"Please, all I keep asking is for you to leave me alone. I don't want to star in the movie you've casted me in anymore. I'm trying to move on, and you won't let me. Please, just let me go." He laughed and that shit scared the hell out of me.

"I will never let you go. Remember that shit. Now that I know where you are, I'll be dropping by more often. I'll be back." The tears fell from my eyes as he leaned in and kissed me. Walking off, he did this sadistic ass laugh and got on the elevator. Forgetting my leg was broken, I allowed myself to drop to the floor and cried my eyes out. Hearing the elevator ding, I tried to get up, but I couldn't.

"How did you end up on the floor? You knew I was coming, so you could have waited until I got here to do whatever it is that you needed." His ass was trying to help me thinking I fell.

"My ex came by and I was overwhelmed. I didn't fall, I just... I just needed a moment. Can you help me up?" As soon as I said that, his entire expression changed. The nigga left me lying there and turned to walk back out of the door. "What the fuck is your problem? Anytime you think there is someone else in my life or someone else does something for me, you throw a tantrum, and I don't get it." I screamed out the door. The way he came back and gritted at me had me scared.

"I don't give a fuck what you do. All I'm saying is get they ass to come over here and help yo ass since they care so much. Why am I the only mufucka in here carrying yo big ass around?" This nigga stayed jealous and I had no idea why.

"You're not my nigga and I don't owe you any explanations. Last I checked, I was single." Shaking his head, he walked towards the elevator. Grabbing the knob, I pulled myself up off the floor. Before I could close it, Mega was charging at me, causing me to flinch.

"Fuck is wrong with you? You're scared of me? Huh, Brielle? You fucking scared of me?" I could see the confusion on his face, and I didn't want him to think it was about him. We had enough issues of our own.

"My ex used to beat my ass all the time, and when people swell up at me like that, I automatically think they are going to hit me. I don't want him and we're not together, but I don't understand why it bothers you so much." For a while, he just stared at me. The shit started making me feel uncomfortable, and I didn't know what to do.

Grabbing my face, he kissed me hard. I damn near lost my balance trying to hold on. His ass had my pussy three-fifty hot and it felt as if I almost needed him. Seeing how I was struggling to kiss him and stand, he scooped me up around his waist. Walking me towards the room, he laid me on the bed and just stared at me. My heart was beating out of my chest.

"I would never hit you. I'm not that nigga and you never have to worry about that. Even when you piss me off, I won't put my hands on you. If you don't know shit else, know that shit." Before I could respond, he kissed me again. It seems like I blinked, and my clothes was off. Within seconds, his face was between my legs, licking the lining off my pussy.

"Wait, should we be doing this?" Giving me a look as if he was ready to fight me, I laughed and let him finish.

"That's more like it, and this pussy tastes good. You know this shit is mine, right?" My answer was to push his head further. I hated when a mufucka tried to have dirty talk; I just wanted the dirt. They could keep everything else. I've gotten plenty of good head in my life, but never any that had me cumming in minutes. When my body started shaking, I just knew I was walking into Heaven's gates. I was still in shock when this nigga got up and sat on the side of my head.

"What are you doing?" Nigga grabbed his big ass dick and started stroking it.

"I love giving head, and I'm good as fuck at it, but it does nothing for my dick. I'mma need some head, lil mama. Get me right, so I can get in them guts." Laughing, I rolled over and gave him some head from the side. I couldn't get a good hold on it, so the shit wasn't going right. "Naw, I'm straight." Mega pushed my head away and grabbed a condom out of his pants. "Your pussy better not be trash like yo mouth." Laughing, I slapped him in the head.

"Don't front me, I got a bum leg. It's hard to get a good angle." Giving me the I'm not sure if that's true look, he continued on with what he was doing. "How are we going to do this and my leg fucked up?"

"I'm a pussy connoisseur. If I don't know shit else, I know how to get the pussy. You just make sure that shit fye." I wanted to get mad, but he smiled, and my shit started leaking. Climbing over me, he held my broken leg in the air and slid inside of walls like he belonged there.

"Fuck!" As if he was telling me to shut the fuck up, he started beating my shit up. Nigga's dick was beatboxing in my shit, and all I could do was scream out. It was a painful pleasure and I didn't know what else to do. His dick was hurting me so good I wanted to dip the shit in bronze and keep it on a shelf. My body started shaking again, and I looked at him, wondering how he would look in a tux. His dick had changed my life.

MEECH...

I was out having a drink; I didn't go to our club tonight because I wanted to do something different. I tried to meet up with my brothers, but both they asses were so-called busy. I knew Mega was sniffing under that bitch Brielle. There is no way in hell I'mma let a bitch get me for my shit, knowingly. A blind man could see that she was running game on his ass, but what the fuck ever. He likes it; I love it.

"Meech!" A voice called out from behind me, and it was a voice I never wanted to hear again in my life. I promised myself if I ever heard or saw this bitch again, I was going to kill her. I turned around, frowned the fuck up.

"Bitch, get the fuck out of my face before I act out what's going through my mind and that's yo hoe ass bleeding out on this cold ass floor!" She knew I meant that shit because her ass was standing there shaking.

"Ummm, I... I'm sorry. I wanted to talk to you and tell you how sorry I am for what I did to you," she nervously spoke, and I pulled my gun out and sat it on the bar. The fuck I look like talking to a bitch that couldn't keep her legs closed. I gave that hoe everything, and she goes and fucks over me. Fuck that bitch! I didn't have to say shit else to her hoe ass, because she got the fuck away from my ass quick. I grabbed my gun to put it back up, and I noticed that bitch Dream sitting at a table with some nigga. I walked up to their table and pulled her ass right out of her seat.

"What the fuck!" Her ass was surprised to see me as she went off. "Dude, why the fuck you got yo hands on my damn girl?" This bitch ass nigga she was with yelled out.

"Nigga, this my bitch tonight. You can have her back when I'm ready to give her the fuck back." Is all I said to his bitch ass.

"Hell nawl! I'm not going anywhere with you. Nigga, you got me fucked up. Ion even know your rude ass." She went on and on with her shit talking, and I was tired of hearing the shit. Her dude tried to approach me, and I sent my fist right into that nigga's jaw. He crashed into the table, and I pulled her ass out of the bar.

"Nigga, get the fuck off of me! I can't believe you did that shit. Ion know why God have to send me crazy niggas. Outta all the niggas in the world, he sends niggas like you. God, I know yo ass punishing me for some shit, but why send this nigga?" She could say what the fuck she wanted. I want what I want, and tonight it's her ass.

"Yo nigga! You think you gone just put your hands on me and walk the fuck away." This nigga yelled, approaching Dream and me.

"Bruh, you gone have to take this loss or take these bullets. I'm not the one to go to war with. I will dead yo ass right here in this fuckin parking lot." This pussy reached for his shit, but I was quicker, sending two shots to his fuckin' chest and pulled Dream to my car.

"Ohhh My Fuckin' God! Yo crazy ass just killed that nigga! Take me the fuck home! I don't want shit to do with no fuckin' murder charge. I only look good in mufuckin' neutral colors; orange jumpsuits never looked good on my ass." She was going the fuck off and talking back and forth to her damn self, but she had the nerve to call me crazy. I guess we some crazy muthafuckin niggas together. I called my homie that owned the bar and let him know the deal. I told him I didn't care what he did with the body, just make sure it wasn't connected to me. Once he told me he would handle the problem, I was good. I knew I would owe his ass for the lookout, and I was fine with that shit. I called Marco because I needed him to go and pick up this bread since I'm gone be held up tonight.

"Yeah." This nigga sounded like he was the fuck sleep.

"Nigga, I know yo old man acting ass ain't sleep?" I had to ask because it was only a few minutes after eleven.

"Bruh, just tell me what the fuck you want." His ass sounded like he was pissed about something.

"I ran into an issue; I need you to go pick the bread up from the spot and take it to the stash." I hope he would agree to do the shit.

"Alright, but yo ass owe me one." Damn, I guess I was gone have to do a favor for his ass. We ended the call, and I looked over at this bitch, and she was fuckin pissed! All I could do was laugh, and that only made shit worse. I pulled in my driveway a few minutes later, got out of the car, and this bitch was just sitting there.

"Man, get yo bald head ass out the damn car." I see now I'mma have to tame her ass.

"I'm not going in there with yo limp dick ass!" Her smart mouth ass yelled.

"This python gone show you some real shit, ain't nothing limp bout my nigga." I smiled, and she rolled her eyes as she stepped out of the car. When we made it inside, I went to the bar and poured us a drink.

"Drink this and shut the hell up, you talk too damn much." I was tired of listening to her ass go off about me killing her dude.

"Nigga, fuck you! I say what the hell I want to say. Your mama should have given yo ass some etiquette classes on how to talk to a woman. Ion even know why I'm here with yo rude ass!" She continued to go off on a nigga, and I saw something move behind her. At that moment I knew she was going to shit. I forgot that I let Lana out before I left home.

"Yo, whatever you do, don't make any sudden moves." Just as soon as I said that shit, she turned and saw Lana! This girl jumped on me so damn quick, crawling up my ass like she was climbing a damn tree.

"What the fuck is that?! You got a fuckin' tiger in this bitch! I'm not staying here. You need to take me home. I knew something wasn't right about yo ass, you fuckin' crazy nigga. God, if you can hear me, I swear I will give up my hoe days and marry me a God fearing man. I promise to stay away from crazy niggas, and big dicks! I pray all these things in yo name!" She was praying and going off at the same time, but had her damn legs wrapped around my waist tight as hell.

"Keep talking shit I'm gone make sure Lana has a good fuckin' meal tonight. Now get down so I can go put her up," I told her, but this damn girl was hanging onto me for dear life.

"Mmmmm mmmmm, nope! I'm gone stay my ass right up here where it's safe." Since she wouldn't get her ass down, I had to walk with her wrapped around my body and put Lana in her room. Scary ass nigga talking all that shit and she

scared of my baby.

DREAM...

"Who was that nigga I had to lay down?" This crazy nigga asked me as he sat down beside me.

"Somebody I finally let take me out and you killed him." I frowned at his ass.

"Yo, you don't have to tell me what the fuck I did. I know exactly what the fuck I did, and I don't give a fuck. That nigga pulled on me, I was just too fast for his ass. If you gone pull yo shit, you better be ready to use that mufucka. cause a nigga like me will lay yo bitch ass in the dirt. The fuck you think this is? I will never let a nigga get the upper hand on me. You got me fucked up, baby girl." He shook his head. I guess I could understand his point, but if he didn't walk up on us like he did, then we wouldn't have this problem.

This shit was fucked up. I wonder what Lenox was gone do when he found out his brother was dead. Damion has been trying to get at me for a while, but I was in a relationship back then. I met him after Brielle and Lenox started dating. He would always try me, but I was faithful to my dude. This shit is fuckin' wild and Bri, is not going to believe this shit.

"Stop thinking about that nigga while you with me, his ass is dead! Mourn that pussy ass nigga when you leave my shit." I couldn't believe the shit that was coming out of his mouth. I heard enough of his shit.

"I'm out. I can't do your disrespectful ass no more. I will call a fuckin uber." I grabbed my shit and headed for the door.

"Normally, I don't chase bitches, but I like yo feisty ass," he said as he pushed me against the door and crashed his lips against mine. This nigga was fine as hell, and the way he was sucking on my bottom lip had my pussy jumping. We pulled our clothes off so damn fast; I guess I was gone be a hoe tonight. The way my pussy was talking, I had to have this nigga. I damn sure hope his dick game was worth it.

"Fuck this pussy wet!" He growled, sliding his fingers in and out of my shit. He grabbed a condom, sheathing his dick, and I swear when I saw that big muthafucka, I was scared shitless.

"Don't look scared now you gone take this dick," he smirked, lifting me up, pressed me against the wall and pushing inside of me with force. I damn near lost my breath; he was fucking me so good. The way he was hitting it, I couldn't remember my own damn name. Shit I couldn't remember shit about my damn self. If the dick was gone make me feel like this. I needed to stay the fuck away from this nigga, but my hating ass pussy wouldn't cooperate, the bitch started moving on the dick on its own.

"That's right, throw that shit back! Fuck!" He gritted, biting down on his bottom lip.

"Ohhh shit! Fuck me!" I moaned as he thrust deep into my guts. I felt my stomach clench and I knew I was about to explode. My pussy muscles gripped his dick, and he continued to bang my shit out.

"I'm cumming!" I cried out. He pulled out of me and slammed back into me. I thought I was losing my mind. He pulled out of me again and bent me over the couch. He slid back inside and went for broke in my pussy. I have never met a nigga that fucked me the way that he was doing.

"Damn, lil mama, this some good ass pussy! Fuckkk!" He roared as he gripped my ass and released into the condom. Before I could blink, my ass was out for the count.

****

The next morning, a ringing phone jolted me from my sleep.

"Hello," I answered that shit just to stop the annoying sound.

"Who the fuck is this?" I pulled the phone away from my ear to see who the fuck this was. That's when I realized I answered Meech shit because it said, Tali Tal.

"I will get Meech for you, one second," I spoke into the phone.

"Mmmmm, mmmm, bring that ass back on this phone. So, you over there fuckin' and sucking on my son lil ass dick, but you can't tell his mama who the fuck you are! I gave birth to that stupid nigga; he wouldn't be able to fuck yo hoe ass if it wasn't for me," she fussed.

"Hoe! Who the fuck is you calling a hoe? I got your hoe!" This lady had me fucked up. Mama or not, I will beat the shit out of that ole lady. "Meech, get this phone. Yo mama got me fucked up!" I spazzed the fuck out.

"Who told you to answer the shit?! Hang up on her ass, a nigga tired. I will call her later." He didn't have to tell me twice. I hung right up on her rude ass. Now I see where the hell he got that shit from. I looked at the clock and it was almost noon. I got out of bed and I could barely fuckin' walk. I don't know how many times we fucked last night, but I'm paying for that shit now. I handled my hygiene and put my clothes on. I had to go talk to my damn sister about last night. He was still sleeping; so I eased out of the room and called me an Uber. About thirty minutes later, I was banging on Bri's door.

"Bitch. why are you banging on my damn door like you the fuckin' police?" I pushed past her, and she shut the door.

"Are you here by yourself?" I had to ask because Mega was always here with her.

"Yeah, why?" She looked at me crazy because I was pacing the floor. I told her everything that happened last night, and she was sitting there with her mouth wide the fuck open.

"You said Damion was reaching for his shit first, right?" Her nervous ass asked, and now she was pacing the damn floor. Well more like limping the floor, because she still had her cast on.

"Yeah, but the fucked-up thing is, I went home with him and fucked the dog shit out of his big dick ass. Now I feel bad because Damion is fuckin' dead." The dick was damn worth it, but my conscience was weighing heavy on my ass today.

"Bruh, you ain't shit! How you gone fuck the nigga after he killed yo date? You gotta keep this shit between me and you. Who is this dude anyway?" Bri questioned, as she sat down.

"His name is Meech, and that nigga is certified fuckin' crazy, but the dick is worth every second of his craziness. I swear, Bri, that shit so good I'm scared to fuck his ass again. Like this nigga got the kind of dick that will make you rob, kill, and fuckin sucker slide yo mama!" I had to laugh at my own damn self.

"Well damn. Mega's brother is named Meech and that nigga is crazy. I wonder if it's his brother that you're talking about." She sat there in thought.

"Ion know, but I know I need to stay the fuck away from his ass. Not because he killed Damion, it's because he murdered my fuckin' pussy. Besides, that nigga got a fuckin baby tiger for a muthafuckin pet. Then his crazy ass got the nerve to call that endangered species his daughter. Nigga I barely fuck with cats. I'm not fuckin walking around his house rubbing and petting on no muthafuckin tiger." I laughed.

"Yooooo, that is Mega's brother! He talks about his brother and that damn tiger all the time." She looked over at me, shaking her head. This shit is crazy. What are the odds that we're fuckin' with brothers?

LENOX...

Dialing Bri's number again, I got pissed as it went to her voicemail. This bitch was gone make me fuck her up. She already know how I get down. It wasn't no such thing as walking away from me. If I wanted that pussy, I was gone get it. Dialing it one more time, I was about to head to her house if she didn't answer.

"What, Len?" Smiling, I started playing with my dick as I responded.

"Why you acting like you don't want a nigga? You know dis dick miss you, right?"

"I know the fuck you ain't on the phone with a bitch while I'm here?" Standing up, I walked over to Dreika without saying a word. Reaching back, I punched her in the mouth and walked in the next room. She knew not to dot that door until I told her to, so I wasn't worried about that shit. Sitting on my bed, I continued to stroke my dick.

"Look, I miss you and a nigga need some pussy. I'm gone stop over there later and check on you." I could hear her take a deep breath.

"Please don't come over here. I don't know what it's going to take for you to understand that I don't want you, but I'm good on that." No matter what I did, Bri always came back to me, so I know it must be some other nigga in the picture.

"Yeah aight." Not saying anything else, I hung up. She was giving that pussy up today whether she wanted to or not. "Dreika, get your ass in here and suck my dick."

Dialing again on my phone, I called Bri's brother, Shawn. His ass fucked over some money of mine about a year ago. I told him then, it was going to come a time he was gone have to repay that debt and his ass was now trying to make good on that shit. I had him working for that nigga Mega, but his ass keep fucking it up every time I gave him a job. I'm starting to think the nigga was doing it on purpose.

"What's up, boss man?" His bitch ass was ass-kissing.

"The deal didn't go through. I'mma need you to force it through. Find a way to steal they product again or some shit. I don't care how you do it, but I need them niggas to need me." Dreika was sucking the hell out of my dick, but she kept trying to lift up. Pushing her head back down, I continued my conversation, ignoring her ass choking.

"They ass been on it since that last fuck up. They don't even let us do the pickups no more. They been grabbing they own bread."

"I don't give a fuck what they been doing. Find a way to get that shit." This time, Dreika started fighting hard to get up, so I let her.

"When I was walking out the door, I overhead Marco saying he will pick up some money for Meech and take it to the stash. He said he was leaving in an hour, so if your boy hurry up, he can catch him." Smiling, I grabbed my dick and slapped her on the lips with it.

"That's why you my bitch, and this dick is yours. Shawn, I take it you know what to do. He is going to pick up some bread and take it to the stash. Find out where that stash is. I want all that shit."

"You think he gone let me rob him and walk away?"

"I don't give a fuck what he let you do. All I know is, you better bring me all that shit, or you can say goodbye to your sisters and that dope fiend ass mama of yours."

"Aight, but we even after this." Hanging up, I grabbed Dreika's head and pushed it back on my dick. I wanted the city, and Mega and his brothers were in my way. The only way to take them out is to make sure they ain't have no money to move shit. I didn't have a crew, and most of these lil niggas was scared to go against they ass. It was a good thing this nigga Shawn owed me, and I had some leverage on his ass. My phone ringing brought me out of my thoughts. It was Bri and them mama, Lola.

"Hey, can you bring me something?" Smiling, I pushed Dreika off me.

"Yeah, I'm on the way." Jumping up, I pulled my pants up and grabbed my keys. "I gotta make a run. You can get up out of here. I'll be gone a minute."

"Can I at least have some money so I can go shopping? I did give you some good ass information." Walking over to my safe, I opened it and pulled out a stack. Closing up, I gave it to her and almost laughed at the expression on her face.

"Damn, this all I get?"

"It's all you're worth. Now get the fuck up out of here before I change my mind." She smacked her lips, and that shit pissed me off. Grabbing her head, I slammed it against the wall. "I keep telling you I'm not that weak ass nigga you with.

I'll put yo hoe ass to sleep without a second thought. Now, get the fuck out of my house before you leave in a black bag." She ran out, and I shook my head as I locked up and jumped in my whip. When I drove off, I checked my armrest to make sure I had a bag on me to give to Lola.

Pulling up to her spot, I jumped out and went inside. She was standing at the door waiting on me. When she reached out her hand, I swatted that shit away. I could tell she was jonesing and needed it bad, but she was gone have to work to get that shit. That was why I left Dreika so fast. Her head wasn't shit on Lola's. I don't know if she was just cold at that shit, or if it was because she wanted the drugs. Either way, she had the best I've ever had. Pulling my dick out, I nodded towards it, letting her know what I wanted.

She immediately dropped to her knees and took it in her mouth. Bri had no idea, but I been fucking her mama since I met her, I had the best of both worlds. A fine ass bitch on my arms and her mama giving met the best head and sex I ever had. Of course, I had to keep that shit on the low because she was a hype, but a nigga was loving that shit. My eyes damn near rolled in the back of my head as she deep throated my shit.

"Fuck, Lola! Suck that mufucka then." Going crazy on my shit, I almost came, but I wanted to feel her walls. Pushing her head back, I turned her around and snatched her clothes down. Bending her over, I rubbed my dick against her asshole and took in a deep breath as I slid in her shit. Lola screamed out, but that only made me brick up more. No matter how many times I fucked her in the ass, her shit was always tight as fuck. Shit was like a virgin times ten. It only took me two minutes to cum all in her shit. When I pulled out, she already knew what to do. Wrapping her mouth back around my dick, she cleaned her juices off me. My phone rung as soon as I handed her the bag.

"What up?"

"The police just found Damion's body! Someone killed him!" My mama was screaming through the phone and my entire body froze. Whoever it was came for the wrong nigga. It was about to get real in these streets.

MARCO...

Grabbing my keys, I walked out of the house and jumped in my Maserati. It was a nice day out, and I would have rather been spending it with my girl. Instead, I was out here doing Meech's job. I didn't go last night when he asked me to go. As soon as I told Dreika I had to make a run, her ass was out the door. Even though I couldn't prove she was doing shit, something was off. Either she was fucking or getting high, but her ass was living foul some kind of way. Grabbing my phone, I called her, but she didn't answer. I dialed her ass a couple more times and same thing. When my phone rung, I didn't even look at the caller ID when I answered. I automatically assumed it was her calling me back.

"Where the fuck are you?"

"If yo lil bitch wasn't out there cheating again, you wouldn't be looking for her like a lame ass nigga trying to find the pussy hole. How you let her get away from you and cheat again?" My mama was going in, and I hated that I didn't look to see who it was. My family would never let that shit go, and I tried my best to make Dreika look like a saint, but shit like this wasn't helping.

"Ma, she is not cheating on me. Y'all gotta let that shit go. We were young and she made a mistake. Shit been good ever since, so for me, can you please stop bringing that shit up?"

"Fuck no. I'mma bring it up until you get it through yo head that she ain't for you. All my sons just out here all wrong. Come by the house. I'mma let Maine talk to you since you not hearing me." Shaking my head, I was glad I was making this run now.

"I can't. Meech need me to pick this bread up for him. I'll hit you up when I'm done."

"You better, don't make me come look for you."
Hanging up the phone, I ran my hand down my face. As much
as I didn't want to, I was gone have to go over there and hear
that shit. Pulling up at the Red house, I got out and went
inside.

"Hey, what up, Marco? I thought I was going to be
seeing that ugly nigga last night."

"He was busy, is it all here?" Passing me the duffle
bags, Feen sat down and pulled out the money counter.

"Yeah, five hunnid big ones. After that shit that
happened though, I would feel better if you counted that shit
up." Nodding, I sat down beside him and started running the
money through the machine. "You heard about that nigga
Lenox?" Now he had my attention.

"Naw, what happened?"

"His ass on a warpath. Somebody killed his lil brother.
He got all types of bounties on a mufucka's head. Nigga

willing to pay anything to find out who did that shit. I ain't no snitch, but if I even think a nigga blew at his ass, I'm getting that bread." Laughing at the shit he said, I shrugged my shoulders.

"That ain't got shit to do with me. We do business with his ass, that's it. I ain't even know his ass had a brother." Feen nodded in agreement.

"Shid, I didn't either, but I'mma act like I know his ass when I'm going for my bread. Be all in that nigga face with fake tears and all." Laughing, I put the money back in the bag and got up.

"Aight, man. I'm out. One of them niggas will be by tonight to grab the next drop. Let me know if y'all need more product."

"Bet." Grabbing the bags, I walked out the door and threw them in my car. As soon as I took off, I tried to call Dreika again. This time she answered.

"Where are you?" I asked while gritting as if she was in my face.

"I'm at the house." She sounded funny, so I calmed down.

"You good? What's wrong?"

"Nothing, where are you?"

"Heading to the stash, I'll be there in a lil bit."

"Okay." For some reason, her voice changed like she got excited, and I felt like an ass. I was steady giving her shit, but she was happy I was coming home, so I was going to cool it on the bullshit I been on. My brother and them been getting in my head, and I couldn't keep doing that shit. Me and Dreika was good, and I needed to believe that shit.

"Aight." Hanging up, I turned my music on and vibed out to the Carter 3. When I pulled up to headquarters, I grabbed the bags and jumped out. Getting home to Dreika was on my mind, so I didn't grab shit else, nor was I paying attention. As soon as I put the code in and my hand on the scanner, a gun was placed to the back of my head.

"I'mma need all that and everything you got inside as well." Cursing myself for leaving my gun in the car, I tried to talk my way out of it.

"I'm sure you not ready to die right now, so I'mma let you gone and walk away. If you try me, it's over for your bitch ass." Praying it worked, I waited for a response. Hearing him laugh gave me my answer. I couldn't put my finger on his voice, but it sounded familiar.

"Nigga, please. You are in no position to tell me anything. If you want to live, you're going to hand that shit over." I dropped the bags, but when I did, I tried to turn around to grab his gun, hoping the bags distracted him. Instead, it scared his bitch ass, and he pulled the trigger. The bullet went through my back and I dropped to the ground. I could hear the guy going in and out the house, so I knew he was getting everything.

All the money we saved up that we didn't put in the bank the entire time we been in the game. Headquarters was securer than the Pentagon, so we never worried about anyone taking our shit. Until now. When I didn't hear him more than ten minutes, I knew he was done. Dragging myself towards the porch, I kept pulling until I got to my car. There was no way I was going to allow the police to find headquarters. With all my strength, I pulled myself into my car. Driving off, wild and fast, I managed to get myself to the hospital. I barely made it out of the car before the pain kicked in, and I dropped to the ground. I couldn't move, and after a few blinks, my ass was out.

****

Looking around, I realized I was in a hospital bed, and there were doctors and nurses around me talking. I tried to sit up, but someone stopped me.

"Hey, Mr. Lucky. I see you have joined us." Looking around confused, I responded.

"Who the fuck is Mr. Lucky? My name is Demarco Storm." She laughed, but I didn't find shit funny.

"I know that, I'm saying you're lucky. The bullet went in and out and missed anything major. We just had to stitch you up and give you some pain meds. You will be fine, just need a little rest. We called your wife and she said she would contact your family." I damn near laughed at that because I knew there was no way Dreika would call them. I guess they assumed she was my wife because I had her down as her emergency contact.

"Aight bet." When they left out, I grabbed my phone and called Mega.

"What's up, lil bro? did you make the drop?" I knew Dreika funky ass wasn't going to call them.

"Nah, some shit popped off, and I got shot. Can't really talk on the phone, so come up here to the County. Call Meech; I don't feel like hearing his mouth. You know his bitch ass gone talk shit."

"On the way." When he hung up, I closed my eyes and Dreika walked in. I could hear her crying, so I kept my eyes closed. My phone started ringing again, but I ignored it. I wanted to see what Dreika had to say. Whoever it was really wanted to talk to me, because they kept calling back to back. After about ten times, it finally stopped.

"You can't die on me, Marco. It's so much more I need from you, and it's not done yet." That was a weird way of asking someone to stay alive. "I need you, for now, so get yo ass up!" That shit caused me to open my eyes and I was ready to go the fuck off.

"Fuck you mean you need me for now? Bitch, you using me?" Her eyes got big, and she started shaking her head no.

"That's not what I meant, Marco. You're always taking things wrong. I need you because you're going to be a father. Maybe I said it wrong, but all I'm trying to say is, we're not done because we have a baby to raise." She looked at me hopeful as I smiled. She saw me leaning towards her and smiled too. As soon as I was close enough to her, I wrapped my hands around her neck and squeezed as hard as I could.

"Bitch, I can't have kids." When I was a teenager, me and Meech got into a fight, and his bitch ass was losing, grabbed a knife, and stabbed me in one of my balls. The doctors told me then I would never be able to have kids. Using all of my strength, I got up out the bed and pulled her towards the door. Pulling all the damn tubes they had in my ass out. I never stopped squeezing and I knew if I didn't get her out of there, I would kill this bitch. I was in a hospital, so there was no way I could get out of that shit if I killed her.

"Marco, wait. Something is wrong. Maybe they were wrong," she said damn near in a whisper, since I was breaking her windpipe.

"Naw, bitch, I was wrong. All this time, I defended yo ass, and they was right. The only reason you're alive is because of where we are. If I ever see yo hoe ass again, I promise I'm going to kill yo bitch ass." Throwing her out of my room, I made my way back to the bed. I was starting to regret that shit as the pain kicked in, hard. Five minutes later, my brothers were walking in talking shit.

"Can't ask you to do one thing without yo dumb ass fucking it up. How you let them get five hunnid thou from us?" Meech was talking shit, but he had no idea how bad it was.

"Naw bruh, they got it all." It was like the room stopped, and no one said a thing. Finally, Meech spoke.

"Mega, talk to your brother and figure out what the fuck he saying because I know he's not saying what I think he's saying. This bitch better not be saying what the fuck I think he's saying." Meech was going off and I knew that they would. This shit was bad, and I had no idea who took the shit.

"Marco, I need you to tell me exactly what the fuck you mean." Mega was trying to stay calm and level headed, but the vein popping in his forehead let me know he was just as pissed. The nigga was gritting on me, but sounded unbothered.

"When I got to Headquarters, I jumped out with the bags. I didn't grab my gun because I was distracted thinking about some shit. When I put the code and shit in, someone was behind me with a gun to my head. I tried to take it and he shot me. Mufucka went inside and got it all." I thought they were about to curse me out, but I never expected them to up on me. Both of my brothers pulled their guns out, and I was shocked.

"Fuck you mean they got everything? What had you so distracted that you forgot yo piece? It's starting to sound like you and whatever nigga got our bread is working together. No one knows where Headquarters is but us, how the fuck was he there waiting on you?" Mega was usually the calm one, but he was throwing accusations at me left and right.

"I don't know, man. All that shit happened so fast, but I swear dude voice sounded familiar." Meech walked by me and hit me hard in the face.

"Nigga, who was it then? You looking real suspect, so I'mma need you to tell me who the fuck it was. Cuz, see, before I came here, I called yo phone ten times my nigga. TEN! Did I get an answer? Fuck no. I was calling to tell you I saw yo ugly ass bitch with Lenox, but I'm starting to think you already know that shit. You're the reason our shit getting hit up." That shit hit me like a brick. Meech had no idea what he just let out.

"Wait, you saw her with who?"

"Nigga, you heard me. Don't try to play dumb now."

"If you don't take them guns the fuck off my child, I will drop both of you where the fuck you stand. Have you lost yo motherfucking mind? Put that shit down now!" My mama had come in guns drawn, and I was happy as hell to see her. She couldn't have come at a better time than this shit.

"Talia, come the fuck down. Yo son got all of headquarters hit and says he didn't have his gun, don't remember who did it, and his bitch was with Lenox." When Meech was done explaining it his way, the shit did sound bad.

"We need to find that bitch. I just threw her out of here because she told me she was pregnant." My mama turned towards me and pointed her gun.

"Naw, son. I'mma need you to tell me what the fuck is going on. Don't leave shit out or it will be the last thought you have."

DREIKA...

A bitch was running up out of that hospital like my ass was on fire. I saw Meech and Mega and hid behind a car until they were inside. As soon as they were gone, I jumped in my car and took off like a bat out of hell. I knew I was never supposed to pop up at Lenox's place unannounced, but I had to let him know what was happening.

Marco never told me he couldn't have kids, and Lenox thought this was a sure way for him to tell and give me everything. Instead, the shit backfired, and now he knew I was lying. All of this was for Lenox to become king, and I was going to be by his side, but now everything was shot to shit. If they knew I had any involvement with Lenox, they were going to come for all of us.

Pulling up to his house, I parked and ran to the door banging as hard as I could. When it swung open, I knew he was not happy to see me at all.

"What the fuck are you doing here? I gave you an order, and you show up to my shit like you don't know the rules." Before I could explain to him what happened, he punched me so hard I peed a little in my panties. I raised my arm to try and stop him, but he was too filled with anger. Lenox grabbed my arm and twisted it so hard I thought he trying to break that bitch. Screaming out in pain, I tried my best to stop him. His ass stomped me as if he didn't know I was pregnant. He didn't stop until he was tired and I wanted to die. "If you lose my fucking baby, I'll kill yo bitch ass." I wanted to scream out how I'mma stop something like that from happening when he just stomped my cervix through my ass, but I didn't.

"I just came to tell you he knows. He said he can't have kids, so he threw me out of the hospital. That plan is no longer going to work," I said it as best I could since my entire body was in pain.

"Why the fuck you didn't say that shit? Bring yo dumb ass inside. Go take a bath or some shit. We will think of a new way for you to get his shit, but for now, you better make sure my baby don't fall out of yo pussy." Nodding, I got up and walked towards the bathroom. It hurt so bad, but I made it in there and ran me some water. I wanted to call Marco and beg him for his forgiveness, but I knew that shit wasn't gone work this time. I cried as I climbed in the tub.

All of this for me to be by the side of a nigga that was trying to be on top when I was already with the mufucka that was. Sometimes, I didn't understand my way of thinking. I had a good man, with good dick, and all the money I needed and I still fucked that shit up. Nothing was never enough for me and I had no idea why. Sliding inside of the tub, I winced from the pain that was shooting through my body. I could hear Lenox on the phone, so I knew he wouldn't come in there with me.

Grabbing my phone, I dialed Shawn's number. When I said I was a hoe out here in these streets, that's what I meant. I was not only fucking Lenox, but I was fucking Shawn too. It wasn't even for the money with him, but his head was like no other. The first time that Marco and them came up short, it was me that took the money. Lenox didn't trust me with it, so he sent Shawn to get it from me. When he showed up, he didn't put on any clothes, so he was standing his ass in front of me in basketball shorts. His big ass dick was flopping around as he grabbed the bags, and the hoe in me couldn't take anymore. I walked over to him and he had no idea what I was about to do. A bitch just dropped to her knees and reached for his dick. I could tell he was scared and thought the shit was a setup, but the moment my mouth hit the tip, I knew he didn't care no more.

Lenox was blowing my phone up, but I couldn't keep his dick out of my mouth. Every time he came, he would take a break by giving me head. It was hours before we actually fucked. By the time I got on top of him to ride that big mufucka, I was drained, and he couldn't stay hard. We laughed about it, he left, and I didn't think anything of it. Lenox was in the dark and kept sending us on runs and shit together.

The first time he sent us to the store around the corner, and before he could pull off, I had his dick in my mouth. I was obsessed with sucking his shit. He pulled over, and I didn't know if I would get the chance again, so I climbed on top of him that time. He came within five minutes, and we went to the store as if nothing happened. After that, I fucked and sucked on that nigga every chance I got.

"Hey, baby girl. You need some of this dick. don't you?"

"Everything is all fucked up. Marco knows that I cheated on him, and Lenox just beat my ass for fucking up. We need to get the fuck out of dodge because everything is about to hit the fan soon." I could hear him cursing under his breath and shit.

"You know if I leave, Lenox will kill my family. I have to finish this and then we can go. We just have to stay out of the way. You can hide out, and I'll do what I need, and then we can go." The tears started falling from my eyes again, because I knew that shit wouldn't work.

"He just told me he still needs me. He's not going to let me go either." We both sat on the phone silently, and then Shawn spoke.

"I'll tell him I don't want to work with you anymore and that I want to do it all on my own. Hopefully, he goes for that shit, and that way, I can protect you. He's not going to let you stay with him because he got too many hoes for that. Just let me think of something to fix it. I'm going to call him and tell him I need you to come get the bread from me. He don't know how much it is, so I'll put some to the side for us. Just get here."

"Okay." Hanging up, I wiped my face and climbed out of the water. I had to pretend I was okay or he wouldn't send me on a run. By the time I was dressed, Lenox was walking in the room with me. His ass was gritting on me, but I had no idea why he was still pissed. He had the money.

"I need you to go get my bread. Just know, if you don't show the fuck up at my door, it will be nowhere yo bitch ass can hide. Hurry the fuck back with my shit." Nodding my head, I kissed him back when he leaned down and stuck his tongue in my mouth. Walking out, I jumped in my car and drove to Shawn's house. What if I said fuck them all? With that much money, I could take off and hideout for the rest of my life. I knew that shit sounded good, but I would have Marco and them, plus Lenox on my ass. Fuck!

Why didn't his bitch ass tell me he couldn't have kids? I thought about what I was going to do all the way to Shawn's house. As soon as I pulled up and parked, he was coming out the door to greet me. Helping me inside, he took me to his room and laid me down. When he pulled my clothes off, I thought he was about to eat my pussy. Instead, he dropped his pants and straddled my chest. His ass knew I was hurt, so instead of making me bend over and suck his dick, his ass leaned forward and fucked my mouth.

"That's right, baby. You don't have to do shit. Daddy will do all the work." Any other time, I would have enjoyed the shit out of this, but not this time. It seemed like everyone, but Marco had a motive for being with me. They all wanted something, and I knew in that moment, I had fucked all the way up. Shit, it was too late, and what's done is done, so I shook that shit off and started sucking his dick the best way I could lying there. Shawn must have needed this nut, because he started fucking the shit out of my face. I couldn't stop myself from gagging, and I damn near threw up. I was happy as hell as soon as I felt his body start to shake.

Snatching his dick out, he stroked it until he came all over my face. Leaning down, he licked his cum and then kissed me in my mouth. I'm sure that was all types of wrong, but it turned me the fuck on. I had no idea who my baby daddy really was, but I was going to stick with the lesser of the evils. As soon as this was over, I was leaving with Shawn.

MEGA...

I can't believe this fuckin' shit; all of our fuckin' bread is gone! I have money in the fucking bank, and some of the money was stashed in a safe that I had in the house, but it was damn near a hundred million in that fuckin' stash house. A lot of that money wasn't in the safe. We had money in different places inside the house. I didn't want to believe that my baby brother had anything to do with this shit, but the shit is just looking real suspect with his ass right now.

"Listen, I know y'all want to blame somebody and get at whoever did this shit, but that's y'all brother lying in that bed in there. Money should never come before your blood." I heard what my mom was saying, but this shit was fucked up right now.

"Man, fuck that, Talia! No one knew where that shit was at, not even you or Pops!" Meech was pacing back and forth, ready to fuckin' explode. I knew our emotions were high, and I try to never act off of emotions. I walked back into Marco's hospital room, and he was sitting there mad at the world.

"Look, if y'all gone come back in here calling me some type of fuckin' thieves, you can get the fuck out. I'm y'all fuckin' brother, and you treated me like I'm just another nigga on the street. I would never take no fuckin' money from my own family. I'm laying here with a fuckin' hole in my back, and the first thing you niggas worried about is the fuckin' money. What about my muthafuckin life? I don't give a fuck how the shit looks. Y'all should be trying to find the niggas that did this shit to me." I knew my brother was pissed, and he had every right to be.

"You're right. My bad, bro. We were wrong, and I promise I'm gone get to the bottom of this shit. I will be back later to check on you. I'm glad you gone be alright." I left his room and headed out of the hospital. When I made it to my place, I found myself in front of Brielle's door.

"Mega, what are you doing here? I thought you were going to be busy tonight?" She looked at me, confused.

"I wanted to see you." I closed the door and followed her into the kitchen. Those damn lil ass shorts and tank top she had on was killing me.

"Are you hungry? I just put the food away, but I can fix you a plate." She smiled, as she opened the fridge, and I immediately shut that mufucka. I was hungry, but food wasn't on the menu tonight, I had a lot of aggression to get off. I pushed her against the counter, attacking her lips and pulling her clothes off. It was just something about this girl that drove my ass crazy. The more I said I didn't want to be in a relationship, the more my mind drifted to her ass.

"Mega," she moaned, as I lifted her on the counter, sliding my finger inside of her wet pussy.

"Damn, this pussy wet as fuck," I growled with urgency as I plunged deep inside of her walls, showing no mercy. This wasn't a night for that slow passionate shit, I was about to get gutta with this pussy.

"Ahhhhh shit! Fuck!" She screamed as she placed her hand on my stomach, trying to push me back some.

"Move yo fuckin' hand! You gone take this dick!" My dick was so damn hard, it felt like it was about to break off in her ass. "Got damn, this pussy good!" I growled as I sucked on her bottom lip and continued to dig deep in her guts.

"I... I'm cumming! Ohhh my God!" She could barely speak the way I was deep stroking her ass. The way her pussy gripped my dick, I knew I was about to lose this battle. I thrust deeper, and deeper, pounding on her spot. Her body began to shake as she came so hard, she damn near pushed my dick out.

"Fuckkkk! The only nigga you gone be fuckin' is me!" I growled as I wrapped my hand around her neck and released inside of her.

"One more thing, Stop calling on that nigga God! He's not the one giving you this dick, I am. I'm a jealous mufucka when it comes to my woman, and my pussy!" I helped her down but meant what the hell I said.

"Your woman? Hmmm... I didn't know we were together." Her smart ass had the nerve to say.

"I'm glad we had this talk, to clear up any confusion you may have had." I smiled, pulling her out of the kitchen and headed to the bedroom.

****

"Yo, that nigga Marco mad as hell at our ass." Even though Meech was always giving Marco a hard time, I knew he felt bad about how we treated him. Even Ma switched on his ass for a split second. That shit wasn't a good look for none of us.

"All I know is, we need to find out who shot our brother and got our bread," I said as I got comfortable in my seat. We were on our way to the stash house to look at the cameras. Meech got a call, and the way the conversation was going, it sounded like it was bad news.

"Fucckk!" I guess it was bad news from his reaction.

"What's up?" I looked over at him.

"The dude I put down last night was Lenox's brother. That was Kareem calling to give me the rundown. They moved the body from his parking lot and dumped it. He said Lenox got a bounty out for information on who shot his brother." I knew he wasn't worried about Lenox, but I pray no one saw him do the shit.

"You sure no one saw you, right?" I had to question him because he needed to be clear that there were no witnesses.

"As far as I know, the lot was clear, but it's a bar, people are always coming in and out." I looked at him and shook my damn head. We pulled into the driveway of the stash house and got out of the car. When we walked inside, shit was thrown everywhere, and money was sprawled all on the floor. I'm sure they dropped the shit because they were moving fast. All the money that we had in the closets were gone. The money in the safe was still there, and the money under the floor was still here.

"How much do you think they got away with?" Meech questioned as he turned the monitors on.

"It had to be about twenty to thirty million in the closets." I gave him a number but wasn't sure of the exact

amount. We started watching the tape and I was fuckin'
pissed!

"Yooooo, this nigga really shot our brother!" Meech
yelled.

"We should have watched this damn tape before we
just accused Marco." It was only one nigga, and he was
wearing a mask. The car looked familiar, but I had no clue
who the fuck this nigga was.

BRIELLE...

It was late when Mega came back last night. I got my
cast off about a week ago, and I was happy as hell. I can't
believe Mega, and I made shit official between us. I loved
everything about him. He was a little rough around the edges,
but he knew how to turn that shit off and on when dealing
with me. I just had to get Lenox to stop fucking bothering me.

There was no way that I would ever go back to his ass. I felt an uneasiness when he came around or called me, and I needed to cut him off completely. I was on my way to my mother's house, and Dream said she would meet me there. It has been a little over a month since we've seen her. I tried to call Shawn, but he's been so damn busy, he has no time for us. When I pulled up in front of my mom's apartment building, there was a car parked across the street that caught my attention. I brushed it off when I heard Dream yelling my name, as she walked up the block. Her car was in the shop so she had to catch an Uber.

"What's up? Did you get your mind right?" I asked her because that shit with Lenox brother had her scared as hell.

"I'm good. After I left you, I stayed in bed for the rest of the day. I still haven't called Meech. I think it's best that I stay away from his dick, and his crazy ass. You know good dick will get you fucked up every time. That python on his ass got

me looking at twenty-five to life! Nahhh bihhh, I'm straight."
She looked at me, and I burst out laughing.

"Dream, you're not going to jail for murder." I laughed
at my sister because she was just so damn extra.

"Bihhhh, you don't know that! All I know is I'm not
fucking with that nigga no more. That nigga got me walking
around scratching and shit like a crackhead. I feel like Lola ass
feels when she trying to get a hit. Mmmm mmm, fuck that. I
want to be regular again. That nigga won't be long stroking
my ass no more. My mind is made up." She was serious as hell
about the shit too. I didn't have time to go back and forth
with her dramatic ass. I pulled my key out and unlocked my
mother's door. When we walked in, we got the surprise of our
lives. I felt like I was going to vomit. This shit couldn't be real.

"What the fuck! Ma, what the fuck are you doing?"
Dream went off, and they both jumped.

"Whhaa...What are you two doing here?" Our mom stumbled over her words. I couldn't believe that she was in here fucking Lenox. This nasty dick, pussy ass nigga, don't give a damn who he stick his dick in.

"Bri baby, it's not what the fuck you think!" Lenox shouted as he tried to grab me. I jumped out of the way; I didn't want his nasty ass touching me.

"So, how long y'all been fucking ma?" I questioned her because this shit didn't just happen.

"I'm sorry, Brielle!" She cried as she grabbed her shirt. That's when Dream and I noticed her fuckin' stomach.

"Ma, what the fuck is wrong with yo stomach? Are you pregnant? Oh, you need yo ass beat for this shit right here! Drugs or not. And this dirty dick, punk ass, ain't shit, nigga needs a bullet in his ass! I swear y'all some nasty mufuckers and you got fuckin' pregnant." Dream looked at her.

"Ummmm... Ain't nothing wrong with me. I'm not pregnant!" She wiped her tears and tried to hurry and put her shit on.

"Fuck that! How fuckin' long?!" I jumped in her face.

"About three years, if I want drugs, I have to fuck him for it!" She continued to cry, and I looked over at Lenox.

"Bitch, stop fuckin' lying before I beat yo ass! Bri, you have to hear me out." Lenox knew damn well the shit he was saying was bullshit.

"Fuck that! This nasty dick nigga need his ass beat and so do yo mama hoe ass!" Dream yelled grabbing the bat that was leaning against the wall. She swung it hitting Lenox ass and I was right there with her punching and kicking the shit out of that nigga. We beat his fuckin ass. He kept trying to grab me and I punched him dead in his fuckin eye. Just as Dream sent the bat crashing down on his back.

"Bitc... Bri, it's not what you think." He tried to explain as he winced in pain. Lola ass was screaming and crying like the bitch she was.

"You not my nigga, but you a trifling ass nigga for this shit. That's my muthafuckin' mama! I'm out of here; y'all can have each other because I'm done with the both of y'all asses." I said what I had to say and walked out of the apartment.

"Bri, on some real shit, she looked like she was fuckin' pregnant! You good because I would still be in there beating they ass," Dream looked at me with a shocked expression.

"At this point, I don't give a damn! Fuck them!" I meant every damn word I said. I couldn't believe what the fuck I just witnessed, and that shit made me sick to my stomach.

"Bri, pull over to that gas station." I pulled into the gas station and Dream jumped out. A few minutes later, she came out with a red gas jug and walked over to the gas pumps. Once she was done, she got back in the car.

"What are you doing?" I questioned her, and she smiled at me.

"Go back to Ma's apartment building." Is all she said and I drove off.

"Is that Lenox car right there?" She pointed at the black Aston Martin.

"Yeah, that's it." Dream jumped out of the car and grabbed the gas can. That's when the shit hit me, that she was getting ready to fuck his car up. I was with all the bullshit today, fuck that nigga! She was dashing gas all over his car. I grabbed a small piece of paper, got the lighter she was holding in her hand, lit that shit and threw it on his car. We watched that shit flame up, and we took off. His bitch ass deserved that shit. I was still pissed but very satisfied.

"Yessss biihhh, we burnt that nigga shit the fuck up!" She laughed, as we high-fived each other. "You better hope our asses don't go to jail for arson." I looked over at her.

"Fuck it, Shawn better come put money on our books." We bust out laughing, and about ten minutes later, I was dropping her off at home. I was so fuckin' pissed that Lenox would even do some sick shit like that. If my mom was pregnant, that would be fucked up on so many levels. My phone was ringing for the tenth damn time, and it was Lenox that kept calling. I had to make some stops and a couple of hours later, I was walking through the door. I was about to jump in the shower when I heard a knock at my door. I peeped in the peephole to make sure that it wasn't him.

"What's up?" Mega walked inside, pulling me in for a hug.

"Hey," I let out dryly.

"What's wrong with you?" I didn't answer. I just walked back into my bedroom. "Yo, what the fuck is wrong with you?" He grabbed me, turning me to face him.

"I went to see my mom, and she just won't leave the drugs alone." I didn't want to tell him all that had happened.

"Everything is going to work out. For your mama to get help, she gonna have to want that shit. Come ride with me, I need to go get some shit from the mall." He grabbed my hand, and we walked out. Being with him is what I needed to get my mind off the bullshit I witness today. A few hours later, we were walking out of the Louis Vuitton store in King of Prussia Mall.

"What's up, Mega?" We heard a voice say, and I knew the voice all too well. My hands began to sweat, and I was nervous as shit. When we turned to face Lenox, his smile disappeared, and a frown appeared. I wonder if he knew it was us that set his car on fire.

"What's up?" Mega sounded as if he didn't want to speak, and his facial expression matched his tone.

"How you doing, beautiful?" Lenox spoke as he stared me down.

"Nigga don't get fuckin' bodied in this bitch! Don't worry about how the fuck she's doing! You talking to me, don't say shit to my girl. You look like you need a doctor out this bitch. Keep testing my gangsta you really gone be fucked up," Mega snapped on his ass.

"Oh damn. My bad, I guess I will let you and your girl finish yo shopping." He smiled and glanced at me before he walked off.

"Let's get out of this mufucka before I catch a case behind that simp ass nigga." Mega grabbed my hand, and we headed out of the mall. I can't believe they knew each other. I know I should tell Mega about Lenox and me, but I honestly just wanted to leave the past in the past. By the way he reacted, there seems to be some bad blood between the two of them. Shit was about to be all bad, and I got sick to my stomach again.

MEECH...

It was a lot of shit going on, and I wasn't trusting a mufucking soul. The fact that they took all our bread had me pissed off. I was ready to light into anyone that I saw. Yeah, it was fucked up that we blamed Marco, but his ass looked suspect at the time, and I wasn't apologizing. I'm not saying sorry for questioning no mufucka at this point. We worked hard for our shit, and if we got booked or killed today, all of it would have been for nothing.

"Nigga, why you looking like somebody died? I'm good and I'm not pissed at y'all; it's good." Marco was always making shit about him.

"Nigga, I know you straight, I'm thinking about my bread. Hurry up and get dressed so we can get the fuck up out of here. I need to find out who got my shit, and I can't do that if I'm sitting up in here making sure yo bitch ass don't die."

"He just talking shit. Mufucka was scared out of his mind when he heard you was shot." I wasn't about to argue with Mega. If he wanted to baby that nigga, that's on him.

"I know. His ass don't know how to express his feelings and shit. That's why he all he does is fuck strippers. His ass scared to lose someone." I looked at Marco and stood up.

"Yeah, that's my cue. Call me when he's been released and y'all take him home." Walking out, I made my way to my car and jumped in. Driving home, I thought about everything that has been going on, and the shit wasn't adding up. We been running these streets for a long time and nothing like this ever happened. It damn sure didn't happen when Maine was running shit. Maybe it was his ass. He did want Mega to stand down since they always bumping heads, but I knew better to accuse him. That nigga would shoot my ass up and wouldn't think twice about it.

Pulling up, I got out and went inside. I could hear my girl whining, and I went in to check on her. As soon as she saw me, she jumped on me and started licking me. My girl missed me, and this was the first time I've been gone from her this long. Getting her to calm down, I rubbed her as she purred.

"I'm sorry, daddy's baby. You missed me? I know you did, come on. Let daddy feed him baby." She followed me in the kitchen as I grabbed some vegetables and shit out the fridge. I barely got them to her mouth and she was tearing them bitches up. "Hey, you better watch my hand." Slowing down, she grabbed them without the excitement and started eating. My phone rang, and I grabbed it and answered.

"Hey, they released him so we heading to Ma's house. She's going to cook and shit, you coming over?"

"Yeah, I have something I need to tell y'all." Mega went quiet, and I know he was trying hard as hell to figure out what it was. I needed to tell them about Lenox's brother and Dream being the reason I did it.

"Yeah aight. I'm telling you now, I'm not for any more bullshit. Hurry the fuck up." I don't give a fuck how pissed he is, his ass knew I didn't play that tough shit.

"You better tone that shit down, my nigga. If you wanna feel yo self, pull yo pants down and go to work. I'll be there in a few." Not waiting for a response, I hung up the phone and grabbed my keys.

"Come on, Lana, you're coming with me, just in case somebody feeling like they wanna do something." I swear if I had known any better I would say her ass smiled.

Walking outside, I looked at my car and I almost turned around. I had never driven her around before, and I was gone beat her ass if she scratched my seats up. Knowing I wanted her with me, I got in the car and prayed she was good. "Baby girl, daddy needs you to lay down. You can't be seen in the car. Oh, and don't scratch my shit." Groaning, Lana laid down, and I smiled. Mufuckas was always talking shit, but my baby listened and knew her daddy. Pulling up at Talia's, I got out and opened the back door.

"Come on, girl." She jumped out and leaped for me. "Down, girl. You're too big for me to carry you. Bring yo big ass in the house." As soon as I walked inside and they saw her, everybody jumped up and grabbed their guns.

"I told y'all he didn't believe I didn't have shit to do with it. Ma, don't let him sick that damn tiger on me." Marco bitch ass was whining and snitching like always.

"Son, I know you in your feelings and it's because you're almost light skinned, so I get that. You a lil soft, but if you think for one second you about to let that lil bitch run amuck in my house, I'm going to kill you and that nappy headed hoe. Get that mufucking big ugly ass cat out of my fucking house." Maine was going off, but I laughed. I knew that was only going to piss him off more, but the threats didn't move me, so I didn't know what else to do.

"You better calm yo old ass down."

"Oh no the fuck you didn't. You not gone talk to my man like he some lil nigga." Mega stopped her from running at me and I just shook my head.

"Y'all doing the shit again. We jumped to conclusions with Marco, and we were wrong. Now, we're doing the same thing to Meech. Let him talk. Find out why the fuck he walked in here with that ugly ass bitch." I couldn't tell if he was on my side or not, but I really didn't give a fuck.

"I brought my daughter with me, because I've been at the hospital all that time, and she missed me. It has nothing to do with y'all, she good and Mega, how the fuck you talking about let me explain, but you still got yo gun drawn as well?" Putting his gun away, he looked at everyone else, and they did the same. "Lana, go play baby girl while daddy talks." She walked out of the room and everyone relaxed a little.

"Now, what's up, son?" Talia acting like she wasn't just ready to tear my head off.

"Look, I told Mega that I was the one that killed Lenox's brother, but I didn't know that's who it was. He was on a date with this chick I wanted to fuck, so I snatched her up. He drew on me, so I laid his ass down." Everybody looked at me like I was crazy.

"Do you know he got a bounty on the killer's head? If that girl catches wind of the shit, what do you think she is going to do? What the fuck were you thinking?" This nigga Marco was a hypocrite.

"Nigga, yo bitch was out there with Lenox. What you think she gone do? Come on, bro, don't come at me unless you ready to catch that shit back. I've killed niggas for less, and y'all know that. Plus, I don't give a fuck about Lenox. I just needed y'all to know what you were dealing with. No more secrets."

"I'm with Meech on this one. Nigga walked up to me basically trying to come at my bitch in my face. He trying to get large amounts of drugs from us, and he had Marco's bitch up to no good."

"It sounds like y'all need to handle that nigga. He has lived long enough. All this shit can't be a coincidence, so his ass is up to something. End that shit NOW!" Maine was barking orders, but I agreed with him this time.

"Hey, I agree and shit, but you do know he would have been dead if you hadn't kept saving his ass? Now, this nigga got our bread and Marco's bitch."

"Fuck you, man!" Marco yelled that shit, but it was the truth.

"Aight bet. That nigga don't get to walk this mufucka. Are we done?" Everyone nodded at Mega, and Talia got up to go in the back.

"Ahhhhhhhh! I swear to God, I'mma kill this lil bitch. Maine, shoot that hoe ass nigga in there. This lil bitch chewed up all my shoes. Get back! You better get yo ass back!" Talia was screaming at Lana, and I knew it was time for me to get the fuck up out of there. Especially since Maine was gritting at me.

"Come here, daddy's baby." When she came running from the back to me, I took off out the door with her. I knew Talia wasn't far behind, and I wanted no smoke from her ass. Now that we handled business, I could go get me some pussy.

DREAM...

Looking at my phone ring, I shook my head again as I declined Meech's call. I wish his good, big dick, fine ass stop calling me. It was getting harder to stay away from him, but I had to. I knew the level of crazy I possessed, and his ass would for sure activate it. I wasn't trying to be out there in the bushes ready to bite his dick in the dark. Not to mention, his mama is disrespectful as fuck. I'm that bitch that will beat her ass then fuck her son over soup and salad.

"Excuse me, can you ring me up? I know you see me standing here?" Looking at the girl in my line, I closed my drawer and removed it.

"I know you see that lane closed sign. Move around." This bitch had the nerve to roll her neck.

"I can't stand these mufuckas that think they doing something cuz they got an Aldi's job. Girl, I'll get them lil ass benefits snatched away." See, I was about to walk away and let her ass make it, but she had to try me.

"No, I can't stand mufuckas that swear they got a bag, but have they ass in Aldi shopping for off-brand shit. If you got so much money, take your ass somewhere else. Girl, you don't know me, and I promise you don't want to. Get the fuck out of my store before I drag yo ass the fuck up out of here." She must have known what was best for her, because she got the fuck up out of there.

I'm glad I was off because I was irritated as hell. Grabbing my things, I walked out of the store and jumped in my car. I needed to check on Bri. I couldn't believe our mama had been fucking Lenox. That means she was fucking him the entire time they were together. Shit was sick, and I swear I wanted to beat both of they ass. I don't care how much drugs you put in your body; you don't do no nasty shit like that. Pulling up to her building, I looked around and made sure I didn't see Meech's bike. Now that I know he is Mega's brother, I had to be careful when I came over. Ain't no telling when I might see his ass.

Jumping on the elevator, I headed upstairs and went to her spot. Using my key, I walked in and she was on the couch watching TV. She had to be watching Grey's Anatomy because she was crying hard as hell.

"Girl, turn that shit off. Have you gone back over there to talk to Mama?" Hitting pause, she turned to me while wiping her eyes.

"I'm telling you that your ass need to watch it, and no, I haven't been over there. It is nothing else for me and them to talk about." Hearing a knock on the door, we both looked at each other. Getting up, I went to the kitchen and grabbed a knife. If it was Lenox, he was about to get his issue today. Bri swung the door open and it was our nasty ass mama.

"Look, I know y'all pissed off, but I didn't mean for any of this to happen. The first time he beat me and made me do it. Once he gave me them good ass drugs, it got easier. The deed was already done. I wanted to tell you, but I knew you wouldn't believe me." I could see Bri softening up and I wanted to slap her.

"It's time for you to go. Don't nobody wanna hear that Dr. Phil ass bullshit. You betrayed your kids for a damn hit off the pipe. Sorry, ain't no sympathy for you here." Bri threw her hand up to stop me.

"Ma, I know you're sick, but that doesn't give you the right to do some shit like that to me. You know better; you just chose the drugs."

"I'm sorry I really am, and I promise to make it up to you. If you can just give me five dollars to buy a bag, I'll do whatever you ask. Lenox won't answer my calls." Scoffing, I walked over to the door and opened it.

"The only reason you brought yo ass over here was because he didn't answer. Get yo ass up out of here before I forget you're our mama."

"Ain't nobody talking to your disrespectful ass no way. I wish I could have swallowed you, but I didn't know you would come out just like yo daddy." I was about to hit her ass when she doubled over in pain.

"Ma, what's wrong with you?" Bri soft ass was getting on my nerves.

"I think I'm in labor." My eyes damn near popped out of my head.

"I knew she was pregnant. This shit gets more fucked up every time you open yo mouth."

"Dream, stop it. This is our sibling in there no matter what she did. We have to help her."

"Girl, that's your sibling and stepchild. I'm not helping her. If you want to be Captain Save A Crackhead, that's on you. I'm done helping her. She crossed a line she can't come back over." Walking out the door, I went back down to my car and jumped in. Driving off, I didn't even bother to look back.

I couldn't bring myself to even imagine how Bri was helping her. This lady fucked your man and was gone fuck him again, but he didn't answer. She's carrying his baby, and now she wants to be there for her. I wish the fuck I would. We did everything for Lola even though she was high. Hell, we were struggling because we were paying her bills trying to keep her from being out there in the streets.

Lenox needed to be shot and I wish Meech had got him instead of his brother. That was another problem for another day. Lenox was on a rampage and willing to pay handsomely for anyone that knows what happened. If I caught wind of the bounty, so did Meech. What if that was the reason he was looking for me? What if he wanted to kill me because I was a witness? That's why I needed to stay away from that killer dick. Knowing his psycho ass, he would fuck me then kill me after.

Pulling up to my house, I parked and got out. I was tired, and I couldn't wait to go my ass to sleep. I was already tired of going to my job every day, but this other shit was taking a toll on me. My ass wasn't built for drama and I wanted no parts of it. My nerves was bad, and my pussy was jumping, and I was gone have to find me another piece of dick. Walking inside, I took my shoes off and went in the kitchen.

Walking to the fridge, I grabbed a bottle of wine and opened it. Taking it back, I took a long gulp and headed towards my bedroom. It was no reason for a glass, because I was about to kill all this shit. I sat the bottle on the dresser and took my clothes off. I saw something move out the corner of my eye, and I damn near pissed on myself.

"Meech, why the fuck are you laying in my bed like you pay rent?" His ass threw the cover off his body and smiled.

"I needed some pussy and you wasn't answering. So, I decided to come and wait on you. I assumed you was busy, so here this dick go. Come get it." Yeah, this nigga was crazy as fuck.

MARCO...

I was ready to murder Drieka's ass. I can't believe that bitch came up in my hospital room talking about she pregnant. I have been staying at my mom and pop's house until I got a lil better. Today was my first day leaving my parents' house. I was feeling a little better and decided to go check on shit at my house. When I walked into my bedroom, shit was thrown all over the place. I looked in Drieka's closet, and she had taken most of her shit out of here. I walked around the room, and the door to my closet was cracked.

When I walked inside, my safe was open, and this bitch had taken all the emergency money I had inside.

"I'm going to kill this bitch!" I shouted to no one in particular. I don't have no words for this bitch. When I see her, I'm fuckin' her ass up. All these years I gave her hoe ass, trusting that she was really down for me, and this bitch wasn't down for me at all. The fact that she was trying to put another nigga's baby on me pissed me the fuck off even more. I wanted all of her shit out of my house. I went looking for a flyer that was left on my door a few months ago about a cleaning service. My neighbor told me they started using the girl and that she was pretty good. Maybe she could help me get the rest of Drieka's shit out of here. I dialed the number that was listed.

"Sparkle cleaning service, how can I help you?" A lady greeted.

"Yeah, I need to set up an appointment to have someone clean and pack up some things for me." It took a few seconds before she responded.

"Yes sir, we can help with that. If you can give me your address, I can come over and take a look at what you have. I will be able to give you an exact quote instead of estimating it," she stated, and I was fine with whatever worked for her.

"That's fine." I gave her my address, and she told me she could be here within the hour. I walked back into my bedroom and decided to lay down until the cleaning service got here. My phone was ringing, and I knew it could only be my brothers or my mama. "Yeah," I picked up; it was Mega calling.

"Yo, you must be feeling a lil better. I just stopped over to Ma and Pops' crib and they said you went home." I knew he was concerned about how I was doing. They were hard on me, but I knew they cared.

"I'm good, just a lil sore but nothing I can't handle. I got some other shit on my mind; I think I should stay home." I knew I needed to tell him about the money Drieka took from me.

"What's going on?" he questioned, and I decided to just tell him.

"Drieka moved her shit out of my house. I guess she knew she couldn't lie anymore with that pregnancy bullshit. She came here and took all of her shit and stole my money out of the safe." Just telling him that shit pissed me off even more.

"So, she is definitely on our radar, and she's fucking with Lenox. That means he may have put her up to this shit, or they're working this shit together. Either way, they ass gotta go. I knew some shit was up with his bitch ass! I know you wanted us to leave you alone when it came to Drieka, but in the end, we only wanted what was best for you. Even though Meech gave you hell about her ass, now you see why. Once a cheating hoe, you will always and forever be a cheating hoe. That bitch was in it for the money and nothing else. Take some time and get yo shit right, we got this shit in the streets. I need you to be on point in these streets, and right now, you not there yet." What Mega was saying was right, I needed to get my shit together, but I needed to know who put this hole in my damn back. That nigga was gone die and that was all I had to say on that shit!

"I need to know who shot me? I can't let that shit ride, bro." I knew he would understand where I was coming from.

"Nigga! We got this, we know the type of car he's driving, and we got people on the streets looking for that nigga. He's gone die; you can put that on my life. He tried to kill you and took our damn money. The only way out of that shit is in a body bag." Mega was pissed. We talked for a lil while longer and then ended our call.

A few minutes later, someone was ringing my doorbell. When I opened the door, I felt my damn breathing slow up. This girl was so damn beautiful, to say her ass was fine was an understatement. I have never had a woman take my breath away and she did that shit within seconds.

"Hi, I'm Jalea from Sparkle cleaning service." She held out her hand for me to shake it, and my dumb ass was standing there stuck until she spoke again.

"Ohh, umm... Yeah, come on in. My name is Marco. I can show you what I need packed up and the things I need for you to clean. The longer I looked at her ass, the more shit I needed to be cleaned. I walked back to my bedroom, and she followed behind me.

"I need all the things in here cleaned up and thrown out. You can take it to a donation site if you would like, but I want it all out of my house. Then I need some light cleaning done in the rest of the house." She looked around the closet and then turned to me.

"Ok, to do light cleaning and to get rid of the things here, it would be about two twenty-five, and I can start now if you want me to." She smiled, and I almost bust one in my damn boxers.

"I'm good with that. Do you need me to get anything for you?" I questioned.

"Nah, I have cleaning supplies in my car." She walked off and went out to go grab her things. All I could think about was deep stroking her ass; the urge to be inside of her was so damn strong. I felt like I needed to tell her to just forget about it and send her ass on her way. I have never felt no shit like this before over no damn woman I just met five minutes ago.

DRIEKA...

Lenox has been calling me like crazy, and I knew if I answered his call, he would be going the fuck off. Shawn and I were counting all the money he took from Marco and them stash. He just took two big duffle bags and dropped it off to Lenox. He told him that was all that he could find in the house, and what Marco had on him, but this nigga had duffle bags and trash bags full of money.

"Fuckkkkk! We got damn near forty million in cash in here!" Shawn jumped up, yelling. I was happy as hell, jumping into his arms.

"Oh my God! We're fuckin rich, baby. We could get the fuck out of here tonight and never come back. We can go anywhere in the world with this kind of money." I smiled at him. I was ready to get the fuck on before I ran into Lenox. I damn sure didn't want to run into Marco or his brothers that would be worse.

"Nah, not right now. I got to act as if nothing is wrong. If I leave now, I will look suspect as hell. I need to take my sisters some money before I get the fuck out of here. I have to make sure that they will be straight. I can't leave them with nothing, and I got money to help them out. I'm giving them both five million. I know they will be more than alright without me being here.

"That's ten million dollars, what the fuck they need with all that money?" This nigga done lost his damn mind.

"Drieka, that's what the fuck I'm giving them. You didn't get this money, I did. Now, if you want to be on some bullshit about it, I can give you five million, and you can get the fuck on too. I love you, but I love my damn sisters, and that's what the fuck it's gone be!" I knew he was pissed, but I just didn't understand why they needed so much of our money. I guess I needed to cool out because he was pissed the hell off at my ass. One thing I didn't need is for Shawn to be mad at me.

"I'm sorry, baby, I was just asking. If that's what you want to do, then that's what we're doing." I kissed him, and he calmed down. I went to the clinic the other day, and they confirmed that I was nine weeks pregnant. The fucked-up shit about is I have no clue who the daddy is. If Marco can't have kids, then I know it's not his baby, but I was fucking him, Shawn, and Lenox.

I know the shit was fucked up, but fuck it! I loved a nigga with a good dick and money. It was different with Shawn. He didn't have a lot of money like Marco and Lenox, but this nigga had a dick on him that was so fuckin' good, I just couldn't let go. If I had to be honest, I had true feelings for Shawn.

"Remember, you need to lay low because I know they're looking for you. We will figure out where we're going and plan to leave in a couple of weeks," Shawn said to me as he packed all the money up and began separating what he was giving to his sisters out.

"I got it. Where are you going now?" I looked at him because I knew he was about to leave me in this apartment all damn day.

"I'm about to go see my sisters and give them this money. Then I have to meet up with Mega and his brothers. They called a meeting with the street team, because of all this shit." He kissed me, put the rest of the money up, and walked out. I was hungry as hell, and I was so tired of eating the shit we had here. I decided to order some food from Door Dash, and it said it would be here in about thirty minutes. So, I decided to take my shower before the food got here.

Just as I turned the shower off and stepped out, I heard the doorbell buzzing. I wrapped the towel around me and ran to the door. When I opened it up, this fine ass chocolate dude was standing there holding my food. He was staring my ass down because he hadn't said a word.

"What's up, shawty? You ordered Door Dash?" He asked, still staring my ass down and licking his lips. My pussy started jumping and that was it for me.

"Yeah, I ordered food, but I would rather have some of you." I dropped my towel and stepped into his personal space, grabbing his dick.

"Ohhh, we on that type of time! I'm always down for a challenge with yo fine ass!" He pushed me back in the house and dropped the food on the table next to the door. He unbuttoned his pants and slid them down. He pulled his dick out and put a condom on, it wasn't big the way I liked it, but he was a decent size. I was playing with my pussy, and he moved my hand, sliding his finger inside my wetness.

"Damn, you ready for this shit!" I turned and got on the couch with my ass in the air. He entered my ass quick, beating the shit out of my pussy.

"Fucckkk!" I screamed, even though he didn't have the biggest dick, he damn sure knew how to use it. This nigga had me screaming and throwing my shit back on his ass.

"Damn, you got some good pussy, bitch!" The more shit he talked to me, the more I wanted his ass.

"Oh shit! I'mma bout to bust!" I screamed, and he continued to pound in and out of me. I came so hard that shit had me stuck. I stood from the couch and pulled him to the bedroom. The way my pussy was jumping, I still wanted his ass, and he didn't seem to have a problem with it. I knew Shawn wasn't coming back no time soon, so I had time to get off with this dude. It's fucked up because I didn't even know his fuckin' name. We fucked, smoked, ate the food that I ordered, and was fucking again. Time had gotten away from us, but the dick was so fuckin' good that I didn't want him to leave. I even gave him two thousand dollars out of the money we had in the closet.

"Damn, girl! I'm about to bust!" Shaheem roared, just as we heard the door open, and Shawn was standing there with his gun pointed at our ass. Fuck! My pussy was always getting me into some shit!

BRIELLE...

Sitting in the hospital, I looked over at my mama while she cried her eyes out. I had no idea what to say to her, and I wasn't trying to find the words to comfort her. She had lost the baby, and she was in here acting like the shit was planned with her husband, and she was devastated. I wanted to tell her ass fuck that baby, but she was my mama, and I tried not to disrespect her.

How the fuck was I supposed to comfort her when she was pregnant by my nigga? All I wanted was to get the fuck out of here, but she needed someone. Dream didn't give a fuck about none of that shit, but we have always been there for Lola, so I couldn't leave her here now. I wasn't sure if she was shaking because she was crying so hard, or if she was shaking because she needed some drugs. Every five minutes, she begged me to go and get her a bag. My ringing phone brought me out of my misery, and I was happy as hell.

"Hey, sis. What's up?"

"Shawn said he needs to talk to us as soon as possible. He said he went by our houses, but neither one of us was home. I told him we would be by later. What you doing?"

"I'm still up here with Ma. She lost the baby and she taking it hard."

"You must be still on them drugs or something. Shit got you acting real slow. If you don't leave her ass the fuck up there and let's go see what's going on with our brother, you better." Dream wanted me to be fucked up like her, but I just didn't have it in me.

"If I leave, she won't have anyone up here. We can go see Shawn later." This time, Dream smacked her lips and went off.

"Our brother, who is always there for us, needs us, but you gone sit yo ass up there with a mufucka who chose a pipe and yo nigga over you for three years. I'mma need you to wake the fuck up, sis. I'm driving to our brother's house to see what's going on with him; you can meet me there or you can hit the pipe, up to you."

"Aight, here I come." I did need a break away from all of this drama, so I could slip away for a little while.

"Ma, I'll be back. I'm about to go grab some food. Do you want anything?" Her eyes got big and she got happy as hell.

"Yeah, two bags and some orange juice." Shaking my head, I didn't even respond. Grabbing my purse, I walked out of the room, and as I passed the nurse's station, I saw Lenox talking to one of the doctors, and I panicked. Jumping over the counter, I cursed my own ass out after I hit a chair and then the ground. One of the nurses looked at me like I had lost my mind, but I put my finger up, telling her to be quiet. Not sure if he was still right there, I whispered to the nurse, trying to see what was up.

"Is he gone?" Looking over, she shook her head, yes.

"You might wanna talk to the doctor next; I'm sure you broke your back the way you leaped over this desk." Standing up, I grabbed my bag and looked around.

"I'm good, thank you." Walking as fast as I could, I ran out to the parking lot and jumped in my car. I said I was coming back, but Lola was on her own. I had no idea if he was still going to be in there, so I wasn't going to take the risk. I wanted no parts of that nasty shit, and him being there only made me feel dumb for trying to be there for Lola. I'm sure she didn't give a fuck about me being there anymore. When I made it to Shawn's house, Dream was already outside waiting on me. Getting out, I walked over to her, and she got out as well. Bitch was walking funny, so I had to stop and look. I had no idea what the hell was going on with her.

"Bitch, why you walking like that?"

"That big dick nigga found me and he fucked my knees inside out. My wig shifted and my cervix upside down. That nigga got sorcery dick, and I don't want it." I couldn't do shit but laugh because she was dead ass serious.

"You the one keep fucking him. Stay away from him if it's like that."

"Hoe, you don't think I tried? I walked in my house and his ass was lying in my bed like he lived there. His dick was just lying on top of the cover, calling my name. Me and yo mama need to be in AA. My pussy was yelling out, 'bitch, don't do it. Look at how that mufucka looking at you, don't do it.' My hot ass didn't listen and now my throat in my asshole, burning like yesterday's chili." I didn't even know how to respond, so I laughed and just followed her upstairs. Dream never knocked on the door, she always used her key that she had to our houses. Doing the same here, she unlocked the door and walked in. His apartment looked tore up and there were bags all over the floor. Walking over to one, I looked inside and saw that it was money in one.

"Bitch, this bag filled up with bread. What the fuck is Shawn into?"

"I don't know, but bitch, all these bags are full of money. I wonder where the fuck he got all of it from. Shid, don't matter to me. Let me gone and get me a cut right now." Her ass started stuffing money in her bra and I shook my head. Grabbing my phone, I tried to call Shawn, but it was going straight to voicemail.

"What if something happened to him because of this money?" Dream couldn't respond because she was too busy stuffing. She was trying to come up, but I was nervous as fuck standing in his place.

"We need to get out of here, girl. Whoever shit this is gone come looking for they bread. You think we should take it and hide it for him?" Thinking it over, I knew this type of money was going to bring the wrong type of crowd. If they came looking, maybe they would let him live if they saw it wasn't here.

"Yeah. When he calls us back, we will tell him we got it, and he can come and get it. Hurry up, bitch, before they come while we're here. I'm not trying to die over this shit." Grabbing the bags fast as fuck, we took them down to our cars and ran back upstairs to get the rest. We did that one more time, and we took off like a bat out of hell. Once we were back at my place with the bags put up in my walk-in closet, we looked at each other, both of us scared out of our minds.

"Do you think they will notice if we went on a lil shopping spree? That's a lot of money. I mean, they shouldn't miss it, right?"

"I'm not touching that shit, man. You trying to die and shit, but I'm good. I just need to know what kind of bullshit Shawn done got his self in this time. He's never done nothing like this before." Grabbing my phone, I called him again, and it still went to voicemail.

"What if they already got him, does this make it our bread?" Dream was trying hard as hell to figure out a way to keep this money, but I felt it down in my spirit that this money was about to have the devil himself knocking at our door.

MEGA...

Feeling something wet on my face, I opened my eyes smiling. I thought I might have fell asleep with Brielle next to me in the bed and forgot, but that is not the case. I was eye to eye with Lana's ass, and she was licking her lips at me like I was her next fucking meal. Slowly grabbing my gun from under my pillow, I pointed it at her, ready to blow her head clean off. I knew my brother loved her, but this pussy was about to get fucked.

"Nigga, you better lower yo shit. You got my daughter over here scared to move. Get that shit the fuck out of her face," this nigga Meech gritted on me.

"Why the fuck you got this bitch in my crib? You know I don't play that bullshit."

"After the shit that happened with Marco, I'm not taking no chances. My hoe go where I go." Shaking my head, I got out the bed and went to the bathroom to piss. I knew my bro was fucked up behind that shit that Dreika pulled and that's why Meech was on edge, but that type of shit happens to the best of us. We tried to warn him, but he didn't want to hear that shit. He thought we were on some hating shit and he had to learn the hard way on who she was.

I wasn't sure if he would be able to kill her or not when it came down to it, but I was going to blow that bitch's head back to the moon. She had me fucked up if she thought she could rob a nigga like me. I know Meech not gone play with that hoe, so it was probably best if we did the shit without him. I know he was still in his feelings, but we had shit to handle and we couldn't be out there dealing with his issues. Walking out the bathroom, I cut the light on to see what the fuck this nigga wanted.

"You talked to lil Carl Thomas?" Looking at him confused, I had to ask.

"Why the fuck you call him that?"

"He's an 'I'm emotional and I can't let go' ass nigga. Did you talk to the bitch?"

"Yeah, he in his bag. I think all of it coming on at one time was just too much for him. We really fucked him up thinking he did that shit to us. Plus, she took the rest of his bread he had put up in the house. We need to figure this shit out quick, or it's about to be fucked up out here for us. One, we gone be broke as hell and two, mufuckas in the street gone think it's sweet."

"Yeah, and the first nigga step to me like I'm a pussy out here ovulating, I'mma lay his ass down. My baby girl will get her first piece of meat out this bitch."

"I'm with you on that shit. Maybe her lil ass can stop staring at me like that. You keep saying she a vegetarian, but her ass want some meat in this bitch." Meech laughed, but I was dead ass.

"She gone get some soon if I don't get my bread back. I know we had a meeting yesterday, but we gone have one every day until we get some answers. I'm laying one nigga down a day." I knew he was pissed, but that wasn't the way to go about this shit.

"We gone figure it out, bruh, trust me. I'm not going out like that. I got a question though, who this lil chick you fucking with?" His ass starting smiling and I knew it was more than a fuck this time.

"It ain't much, man. Just somebody I met at the strip club." Now I was gritting on his ass.

"You telling me you killed Lenox's brother over a fucking stripper? Are you fucking crazy?" When he called Lana over to him, I couldn't do shit but laugh.

"Naw, she was at the table next to me cursing they ass out. She fucked my boo up and that shit turned me on. Next time I saw her, she was downstairs outside yo building, and I gave her my number. You know I ain't on no relationship shit, but I like her smart mouth ass. Shit makes my dick hard."

"Meech, I don't want to hear about yo fucking dick. Fuck wrong with you my nigga? You like shorty, you just don't realize that shit."

"I'm not you, and I don't fall for every bitch that smile my way. That's how you end up with a bitch like Dreika. Sucking yo dick and stealing yo bread. I'm good on that shit."

"Won't be me either. Hold on, you said she was here? Why the fuck was she in my building?" His ass started looking dumb and he didn't have the answer.

"I don't know, but now that you mention it, shit is suspect. She's never said shit about coming over here again. If that bitch know that nigga Lenox, I'mma kill her ass tomorrow." Now I was lost.

"Why tomorrow?"

"Cuz I'mma need some pussy one mo' time. It took me a long time to find some pussy like that, I can't let it go that easy. Man, I can't be out here under the Marco act. Both of us can't be the dumb niggas out the crew." His ass was worried about the wrong shit. Then it hit me.

"Bro, she was with you when you killed Lenox's brother?" His eyes lit up, and he knew exactly what I was getting at.

It seemed like everything always came back to that nigga. I hated I listened to Pops ass and let him breathe this long. Mufucka wouldn't have had a chance to do none of this shit if I had followed my first mind. Something about that nigga rubbed me wrong, and Meech was the only one down with me airing his bitch ass out. Now that shit was coming back to bite us in the ass.

This nigga found a way to infiltrate us, but I never thought it would go down like this. He had found a way through each of us, which left me to wonder how he was gone try to get to me. Not to mention, if she saw him kill his brother, shit was about to get all bad for baby bro.

"You know he about to be coming after you, right? There is no way he doesn't know it was you. He's trying to figure out a way to bring it to yo ass."

"He can try, but I ain't going out like a bitch. Both they ass got me fucked up." The door swung open, causing both of us to jump. It was Marco and he was looking crazy as fuck. I didn't know if he was losing his mind or if he was having a bad day, but either way, his ass looked a mess.

"Fuck wrong with you? In here looking like Harpo lying. 'It was a Mule Pa. I swear it was a mule' looking ass. I wouldn't even want a mufucka to know a bitch had me out here looking like death." When Marco didn't respond, I knew it was something serious.

"Bro, what's up with it?"

"I figured out the voice. I know who shot my ass and we was right, he in our circle." This nigga paused for dramatic effect.

"Who, nigga? Damn. Slow droopy lip ass." Meech was getting impatient and so was I.

"It was Shawn." Thinking back on the car, I knew he was right. Nigga pulled that shit off right up under our noses.

DREAM...

I had been calling my damn brother for the last couple

of hours. Ion know where the fuck he got all that money from,

but a bitch was about to go shopping. It was so much fuckin'

money in those bags he wouldn't know that a few stacks were

missing. Bri could play around all she wanted, but Shawn was

our brother; he wouldn't care. I just hope he knew what the

fuck he was doing, and not jeopardizing his life over this shit!

What the fuck is going on with my family? Our mama

a hoe, our brother a thief, and Bri ass is just too damn slow for

acting. I'm telling you now I would have given Lola ass the

fuckin' business. I'm done with her ass; I'm not paying

another muthafuckin' bill for her. She can figure that shit out

on her own, fuck that! My phone was going off and it was

Meech crazy ass. I made up in my mind that I'm not fucking

with his ass no more. I was still trying to figure out how that

nigga found out where I lived and got into my shit. See, that's some stalker type fuckery, and I don't have time for that shit. My phone was going off again, and this time it was Shawn.

"Bro, where the fuck are you?" I asked as soon as I hit the answer button.

"Sis, I done got myself into some bullshit. I need for you, Bri, and mama to go get a room and stay low until I try to get out of this shit. Don't tell nobody where the fuck you're going, Nobody Dream!" He sounded nervous as shit.

"That's a negative on yo mama hoe ass. I will explain that shit later. Where did you get all that money from Shawn? What the fuck is going on?" I questioned just as I heard banging on my door.

"How the fuck you know I got money?" He snapped with that question.

"Because me and Bri came over to your place and there was money in bags. We didn't know what kind of shit you were in, so we took the shit and hid it at Bri place." He sighed and seemed to have calmed down a lil bit.

"Fuck! I thought the niggas I took it from had found out I took the money. These niggas are nothing to play with, and I'm leaving the city. I don't know where I'm going, but ten million of that money belongs to you and Bri. I came to give it to y'all last night. Another thing stay the fuck away from Lenox, that nigga is crazy, and a lot of shit that I did was to protect Bri. I just need y'all to lay low and tell Bri that I'm coming to pick the money up. Just make sure she gets the money out for you and her, I love you and will call y'all soon." He ended the call, and the knocking on my door continued along with my phone going off. It was Meech calling again, and I decided to pick up so he would stop calling.

"Yeah, nigga!" I snapped.

"Yo, come open this fuckin' door before I shoot the lock off this bitch!" This nigga was indeed crazy. I'm not letting his crazy ass in here, and he's threatening me. Fuck

that! Ain't that much good dick in the world. These bitches be

falling out when a nigga got some good pipe, but I love my

fuckin life more.

"Nah nigga, we done. Yo ass too crazy for me! Go find

one of them hoes that don't give a fuck about a nigga that

needs a crazy check." Just as I said that the nigga started

kicking my door again.

"You got sixty seconds to open this fuckin' door!" He

was mad as hell, and it was time for me to get the fuck out of

here.

"You better leave me the fuck alone before the

neighbors call the cops! Look, we had a good time with each

other, but I don't need the type of drama you bring. I can't be

strung off a good dick, crazy nigga, and I'm allergic to jail!" I

said to him, hoping that he would just leave. Lawwwd, I

knewwww I should have kept it moving and not open my legs

for this fine, crazy nigga. I always attract the insane mufuckas.

He didn't say shit else, so I just hung up on his ass. I

went to my closet and started packing a bag. Normally, I

would give Shawn a hard time when he was trying to boss us

around, but the way he sounded on the phone I think it's best

that we listen to him. I knew Bri was going to be the one

giving me a hard time about going to a hotel. She was too

stuck on that nigga Mega, he dickmatized her ass and now

she gone off the D.

When I walked out of my closet, I heard gunshots. I hit

the floor fast as hell, almost pissing on myself. I know I'm in

the hood, and gunshots are always going off, but that shit

sounded close as fuck. A few minutes later, Meech came

walking in my room, with his gun out leaning on my dresser.

Ahhhhhhh fuck! I done fucked the devil. Nahhhh, scratch

that, I think this nigga is worse than the devil. Like, who

shoots a bitch crib up just to get in it? Ion even want no more of the dick! But what took the cake for me, is when I saw who was standing beside him. That was it, I fuckin' lost it! This nigga had that fuckin' baby death wish on legs with him.

"What the fuck are you doing? Nigga, you need to go see somebody about your fuckin' craziness. I'm telling you, yo ass can get a fuckin' check, and I'm about five seconds from calling animal control. You and that hoe gotta go!" I was on top of my bed, scared as fuck. He looked pissed, and so did his muthafuckin' sidekick.

"So, you thought you were gone stop fuckin' with me?" he was giving me a death stare.

"I can't keep fucking you, we not going nowhere with this shit. I swear the dick good, it's some of the best dick I ever had, but you're going around breaking in my house, shooting a nigga, and now shooting your way in my shit! Hell no, the dick just ain't that good." He pushed away from the dresser and moved to the bed, reaching out for me. I was gonna make a run for it until I realized Machlie the third was waiting on the other side of the bed for me. Meech snatched me up and crashed his lips into mine.

At first, I fought him, but when he slid his hand inside my panties, my pussy was on fire. Fuckin' bitch, I hated when her ass traded on me for the dick, that hoe was a fuckin trader. I hate when her bitch ass don't be on the same page as me.

"So, you were gone leave a nigga? You not gone stop fuckin' with me, until I say stop fuckin' with me. I'mma make yo ass pay for trying to not give me no more pussy!" This crazy nigga growled and ripped my damn shirt off.

"So, you just gone fuck me with yo human eater sitting there watching us?" I looked from him to that beastly hoe.

"Hell yeah, my baby like watching," he spoke as he slammed into my pussy, and I screamed for dear life.

"That's what the fuck you get for trying to get ghost on me. With this good ass pussy!" He roared and slammed into me again.

"Ohhhh fuck!" I screamed, as my pussy started creaming all over his ass. He was straight dog walking my ass, and my pussy was sucking his ass right on in. This dick had my ass spazzing the fuck out. I tried to move, but I was no match for what he was doing to my ass.

"Get on this dick and ride this mufucka." He laid down, and I crawled on top, easing down on his dick. I began moving up and down on it. I had to gain my composure to show this nigga who he was fuckin with.

"Fuck girl!" He growled as he gripped my ass cheeks trying to control my movements. I smacked his hands down and fucked the shit out of his ass. Just as I was about to cum, Bri was calling my name running into the bedroom. She damn sure got an eyeful because neither one of us stopped to acknowledge her ass.

"Really Dream! Ohhh My God, is that a tiger?" She shouted, slamming the door, just as Meech and I were both cumming.

"Yooo, was that Bri?" He questioned, as I climbed off him.

"Yeah, that's my sister." He looked at me and burst out laughing.

"What's wrong with you?" I knew why he was laughing, but I had to ask just to play it off.

"You know she fuckin' with my brother right?"

"Nah, I didn't know that Mega was your brother." I looked at him, and he shook his head.

"Damn! Do you know a nigga named Lenox?" I thought about his question and wondered why he was asking me that shit. I mean, I know he killed Lenox brother, but I needed to play it smart.

"No, I don't know nobody named Lenox. Why you ask?" I needed to protect, Bri, because I don't know if she told Mega about Lenox ass or not.

"The dude you were with was his brother, and I thought you knew the nigga." I think he was trying to figure some shit out.

"I don't know anybody from his family, that was the first time I met up with him. Now get your beast, so I can go get in the shower." He stared at me for a minute and got up to guide me in the bathroom. He followed behind me and we jumped in the shower. About thirty minutes later, we stepped into the living room, and my sister was gone.

MEECH...

I had to laugh at the thought of Dream scary ass, trying to cut me off as I walked in my door. I meant what I said, the shit wasn't over until I said it was the fuck over. The way I'm feeling that shit won't be anytime soon. I was shocked to know that Dream and Bri were sisters. Now I know why I ran into her ass at Mega's building. It was just too much shit happening for me.

I can't believe that this nigga Shawn ran down on my brother, and took our fuckin' money after we gave that pussy a chance to fix the shit from the last muthafuckin' robbery. Now that I think about it, them niggas were behind that shit. Ain't nobody robbed their asses. Grabbing my ringing phone, I peeped that it was Mega.

"Yeah," I spoke into the phone.

"I got the info we needed on that nigga Lenox. We move on his bitch ass in a couple of hours." I knew my bro wanted that nigga's head. He never liked his ass.

"I'm ready whenever you are. You ready for your party? I can't believe your old ass about to be thirty in a few days, nigga!" I laughed, because Mega was not feeling this party shit. He said he would rather spend time with his family, but we convinced his ass that it was going to be just a few of us. I fuckin' lied. We're going all out for big bro. The turn up was going to be a muthafuckin' night to remember. I hope his bitch don't get mad; it's gone be a pussy fest 2020 in that mufucka!

"I'm ready to embrace it, we're all getting older and I'm looking at life differently. It's time to put certain things into perspective. Bri and I made shit official." This nigga said, and he sounded soft as hell right now.

"Hell Nawl! Nigga, you done got bit by the pussy bug. You're sounding like a lil bitch right now. You gotta tighten up! Don't let the pussy get yo ass. That shit is a setup. I think these bitches have a way of knowing how to lock down on the dick to drain your soul out with the cum. They ain't getting' my ass. Just as soon as I feel my soul trying to creep out, I internally cuss that nigga out and we cool again!" Fuck that, I can't get got.

"Nigga! You do know you're batshit crazy, right? I'm telling you now, you may think you got control over your heart, but somebody is going to come along and knock your rude ass off your feet. You're not gonna see that shit coming. Bri is it for me; everything about her feisty ass is what I need. I think I love her, bro, and I want her to move in with me."

"Ahhhh, fuck that! Hold the fuck on!" This nigga needed an intervention, and I needed help with this nigga.

"What's up?" Talia questioned when she picked up. I merged the call and adding her in with Mega and I.

"Talia, yo son over there talking crazy. He said he thinks he in love and wants Bri to move in with him. You need to talk to the nigga!" I filled her in, and she was laughing hard as hell.

"Nigga, you do know that I'm grown as hell, right? Calling my mama on me ain't gonna change shit." He laughed, but I didn't see shit funny.

"Awww Mega, you love her? I love her for you. She doesn't get on my nerve like the rest of them bitches y'all be fuckin' with. Especially that bitch Meech fuckin'. When I see her, I owe her ass a beat down." Talia fussed, and I couldn't believe what I was hearing.

"Oh yeah, the chick I told you about is Bri's sister. I was over there trying to get my shit off, and Bri walked in on us." I forgot to tell his ass that shit.

"Nigga, you fuckin' with Dream? Man, leave her alone. She a cool girl, and I know yo ass ain't gone do right by her." He knew how I operated.

"I sure hate that I got to put these paws on her ass. Maybe I will just beat her body up instead of fuckin' her face up," Talia crazy ass said.

"Talia, you not putting yo hands on my bitch! You gone have to take that one on the chin my nigga." There was no way I was gone let Talia fuck with Dream.

"Ohhhhhh, wait a muthafuckin' minute. Nigga, you over here complaining about yo brother, but it sounds to me that the almighty *they call me Big Meech, Larry Hoover* lookin' ass nigga, done got pussy whipped!" Talia sang, quoting Rick Ross song and then burst out laughing.

"Ma, I think you might be right. This nigga said you not touching his bitch!" This nigga Mega laughed, and I just hung up on both they asses. I'm not fuckin' pussy whipped. The bitch just got some good pussy, and she was finer than a mufucka. Just thinking about her wide hips, big ass, and them double D's got my dick rock hard. I picked up my phone and dialed her up.

"What? You better not have your ass at my door trying to shoot my shit up again!" Her shit-talking ass always had some smart shit to say.

"Yo, shut that shit up! Come here, I need you to handle this hard mufucka for me." I know her ass was about to go off.

"Nigga, you act like I'm there with you. That's not how you talk to me. I'm sick of your disrespectful, rude, crazy ass talking to me like that. I'm good on you. I'm gone find me a nigga that knows how to treat a woman. When God made good dick, he didn't just give it to your ass. I'm sure there are many good dicks in the world, and send somebody to fix my door." This chick was gone make me fuck her up.

"Bit...Dream, if you value yo life and the nigga you plan on fuckin', it's best that you don't fuck with me. You and that nigga will be dead before you could think about sliding down on the dick! I might even cut yo pussy out and hang that bitch on my wall. That way I will never be without it. Now get yo ass over here and hop on this dick! If you not here in thirty minutes, I'm coming to get you, and we both know you don't want that shit." I hung up and hopped in the shower after I called a cluck to go fix her shit..

I think I'm gone fuck her brains out until it was time to ride out later. Damn, I can't believe that I really wanted this bitch that bad. I never fuck with the same bitch twice; I need to get my shit together. I was in the shower, and I heard my doorbell ringing. I jumped out, dick swinging and walked to the door. When I opened it, her nasty ass instantly looked at my dick. I pulled her inside and walked back to my bathroom.

"Take yo clothes off and get in with me." I smirked because she moved so damn fast to get her fuckin' clothes off.

"Why you always threatening me?" She questioned, as I pushed her ass to the shower wall.

"Why yo ass always got some smart shit to say?" I stared her down, and the way she looked at me woke up something inside of me. My heart was beating like crazy, and I couldn't control the feeling. I crashed my lips into hers, sucking the hell out of her lips; this kiss felt different. I even had the urge to taste her pussy, and that was some shit I don't do to these bitches. My ex, Tasha, was the last pussy I ever wrapped my lips around. It was just something about this chick that had my ass ready to suck her damn uterus out and sit that bitch by the shampoo. Sliding my fingers inside of her, that shit was wet as hell.

"Ahhhhh, shit!" She moaned, and I lifted her up enough to where her pussy was in my face. She held onto me, wrapping her legs around my neck. Her body began to shiver, as I slid my tongue across her clit and latched on.

"Yess! Lick this pussy nigga!" She cried out, and I went to work, sucking and licking on her clit. Her shit tasted like pineapples and strawberries.

"Damn!" I mumbled, and her body started to shake. I knew her well enough now to know that she was about to cum. I slid my tongue inside of her pussy, latched onto her clit, and suctioned that cum right up out of her ass.

"Ahhhhhhh, fuck!" She cried. I mean, she had real fuckin' tears streaming. The crazy part about it was, I was pissed the hell off that she was crying. Almost as if my heart never wanted to see her cry. I slid her down halfway and entered her, fucking the shit out of her. It was as if my dick and I felt at home inside of her. I found her spot and pounded on that shit over and over again.

"Fuck me! Fuck the shit out of me!" She groaned as she gyrated on my dick.

"I'mma about to cum, you gone take this dick, and stop trying to fuckin' leave me. You give this pussy to another nigga, I swear...Ohhhhh, fuck! I swear I'm killing yo ass!" I yelled and we both bust at the same time, filling her ass up with all my damn seeds. That shit hit me like a ton of bricks, I didn't wrap the fuck up and I just came all inside of her ass.

Fucckkkkkk! We walked to the bedroom and my ass was out like a light.

Later that night, I was in the car with Mega. We were following this nigga Lenox, trying to wait on the best time to open fire on his bitch ass! Because tonight would be his last night amongst the fuckin' living.

LENOX...

My only fuckin' goal is to find out who killed my fuckin' brother. I had a half a million out for information on the niggas that killed him. I was on my way to drop Lola ass off at home. I knew fuckin' with her was gone get me caught the fuck up. There was no way that Bri was gone ever get back with me now. I fucked up, and I knew the shit looked bad. I loved Bri, but her mama just had some good pussy. I can't believe they whooped my ass and set my fuckin' car on fire.

Both of them bitches lucky I didn't tell the cops they fuckin' did that shit, but I wanted to handle that shit on my own. I'm gone kill that bitch Dream and after Shawn did what I needed him to do, I'm killing his ass too. I wanted to choke the shit out of Bri, when I saw her with that nigga Mega. I'm gone make sure I fuck her hoe ass in front of that nigga, right before I kill him.

"Len. you gone give me some money to pay my bills? My kids not gone help me no more." Lola was beginning to be a pain in my dick. She knew damn well her ass wasn't gone pay any damn bills. I swear I don't know how the fuck I got attached to her crackhead ass.

My phone was going off, and it was that bitch Drieka. I have been calling her ass for a few days and she hasn't answered none of my calls. I was beating her ass when I saw her.

"Where the fuck you been?" I didn't have time to be nice to her ass.

"I have been sick; you know I'm pregnant with your baby. I need you to come and pick me up. I don't have nowhere to go, and Marco is going to kill me. I can't be out here roaming around; they might find me," she cried. I should leave her ass out there.

"Give me thirty minutes, and I will call you back." I hung up on her ass. I pulled on Lola block, pulled my dick out and she smiled. Adjusting my seat, I pushed her down so she could give me some head. Out of nowhere, gunshots rang out, and bullets were hitting my car the fuck up. I grabbed Lola and threw her over my body using her as a shield and the bullets lit her ass up. I didn't give a fuck about that bitch. I was trying not to get shot. I did take one in the arm though. The gunshots ceased and the car that sped off looked exactly like that nigga Mega's car.

"Fuckkkkkkkk! Them niggas really just tried to take me the fuck out!" I yelled out to myself. I quickly pushed Lola out of my car onto the ground and sped off. I needed to get my car to my homie's shop so they could burn that shit.

A couple of hours later, I had one of my nurse friends I was fuckin' come over and pull this damn bullet out of my arm. These niggas wanted to play; I was ready for fuckin' war! I grabbed my phone and dialed up Shawn bitch ass.

"Yeah," he answered like he was sleep.

"Nigga, get the fuck over to my crib now!" I hung the fuck up. If he knew what was best for him, he would get the fuck here. About fifteen minutes later, I heard a knock at my door. I opened it up, and Shawn stepped inside.

"What's up?" This nigga had the nerve to question me with an attitude.

"Nigga, lose that pussy ass attitude. I need you to find out where the fuck that nigga Mega, and his brothers live. Them bitches shot at me and they gone pay for that shit. I need you to bring me all the bread you got from them niggas!" I knew this nigga kept some of that money he got out of that stash house. I don't know who the fuck he thought he was dealing with.

"Nahh, nigga. I'm done with this shit. All the shit I did for you I paid my debt to you off by now. I'm not fuckin' with them niggas. The more I fuck over them, the more I put my life in danger!" I had to laugh because this nigga really thought he called the shots.

"Nigga you ain't done until I say you done. I will make sure when I kill yo bitch ass sisters, I'mma take my time and fuck they fine ass first. If you want them bitches alive and untouched, you gone do what the fuck I say do! Now get the fuck out and get me what the fuck I asked for!"

I'm done playing with his simple fuckin' ass. The nigga shouldn't have come to the devil for help if he didn't want to play in hell. I grabbed my phone and I saw that I had ten damn missed calls from Drieka ass. I texted her ass because I didn't feel like hearing her voice. She sent me her location and I went to go pick her ass up. When I pulled up to the diner on Roosevelt, she hopped in my car and I punched the shit out of her ass.

"The next time you try to hide from me bitch, I will kill yo ass!" I punched her ass again and drove off.

"I'm sorry," she cried like them fuckin' crocodile tears were gone work on me.

"You better not get no blood on my damn seats!" She lucky my baby was inside of her ass. My phone was going off, and Drieka looked over at me, sucking her damn teeth. I grabbed my phone answering the call.

"Yeah." It was from an unknown number.

"Hello, I'm calling about the information you're looking for on your brother." I sat up in my seat.

"Yeah, what you know about that?" I questioned to see if she really had some information.

"I know a lot about it, I saw it all go down, and I know who killed him." I almost ran off the damn road. If she knew who killed my brother, I needed to know that shit now.

"What's your name, baby girl?" She didn't answer me right away.

"My name is Tasha. Is the bounty still a half a million?" She asked, and I damn sure would give her that shit if she had something viable.

"Yeah, I got you. Meet me on City Ave at the Crowne Plaza in about twenty minutes," I told her as I pulled in my driveway. Drieka ass was steaming mad because she thought I was going to a hotel with a bitch. I'mma let her keep thinking that shit.

I ran into the house, grabbed the money I needed to give this girl and jumped back in my car. By the time I pulled up in the hotel parking lot, she said she was parked near the entrance. I spotted the car she told me she was driving, and I pulled up right beside her. She got out and hopped in with me.

"Tell me what you know, the money is in that bag." I didn't feel like beating around the bush.

"This guy I used to date, his name is Meech, he is the one that killed your brother. He seemed as if he was mad about your brother being in the bar with this girl. He grabbed the girl up; he and your brother had some words and they walked outside. I decided to follow and kind of stay out the way. They were going back and forth, and the next thing I knew, gunshots were fired and your brother hit the ground. Meech and the girl jumped in his car and sped off." I knew I was going to kill this nigga, but I'm going to make his bitch ass suffer.

"You know where he lay his head?" I asked to see if she had information on where this nigga lived.

"Nah, he moved after we broke up, but I'm telling you he's the one who did it. Before you kill him, make sure he knows I told you he did it." She smiled, grabbed the bag, and got out of the car.

I quickly dialed up Shawn because I wanted this nigga to understand if he didn't get me what I needed I was killing all their asses. I didn't have to worry about killing Lola because her ass was already dead. It's fucked up she had to die. I was gone miss that pussy and head game she got, but it was either her or me and it damn sure wasn't gonna be me.

"Yeah!" He yelled in the phone like he was supposed to scare me.

"Nigga, you need to make sure you get that information for me. I just found out that Meech is the one that killed my muthafuckin' brother, and I want his ass. As a matter fact, get me that fuckin' information tonight! I know you know somebody that can tell you where them niggas live at." I knew he knew more than what he was giving me.

"I just found out that Mega is having a birthday party at club Haze Saturday night. If you want all them niggas, that's the place you will find them at. Now, leave me and my sisters alone. Don't call my fuckin' phone no damn more. My debt to you is paid off nigga!" This pussy hung up on me. I think when I handle these other niggas, I'm gone kill his ass for sure. It's one thing I hate, and that's a pussy ass nigga, and Shawn was definitely a pussy. That nigga debt was done a long time ago, but he loved his sisters, and I knew telling him that I was going to kill them bitches would get him to do whatever I needed.

There was nothing that was going to stop me from killing these niggas. I wanted their ass dead so bad; my damn dick hurt! At this point, I'm ready to murder their whole damn family. They got my mama and sisters out here in pain from losing my brother. Now that I knew where they were going to be, I got a party to attend. I promise everybody that's connected with them niggas is gonna pay with their fuckin' life!

MARCO...

Everything that had happened at this point had us side eyeing the fuck out of everybody. Jalea was a cool chick and I even took her out on a few dates, but I couldn't bring myself to trust her. After that shit with Dreika, I felt like being on my Meech shit. That nigga didn't give a fuck about a chick's feelings and maybe it was time I started being more like him. It was gone be hard because I was one of those niggas that loved being in love. Me and Dreika had our problems, but I was a good ass nigga.

Even though we were good now, shit still didn't sit right with me that family kicked me when I was down. Yeah, we rectified that shit by laying that nigga out a few days ago, but I still wanted the nigga that put a hole in my back. It seemed that everybody only cared about the party and forgot it was still a nigga out here we needed to handle. Yeah, I was big mad and in my feelings, but they ass took something from me. My bitch, my trust in bitches, and a chunk of my fucking back. Usually me and my brothers were always together, but if we weren't conducting business, I stayed to myself. I know I was being a bitch about shit, but them niggas upped on me and I will never forget that shit. Hearing growling, I turned around and was face to face with Lana. Jumping on the couch, I grabbed my gun and started screaming.

"Maaaaa!!!" She came running in the room, but when she saw it was Lana, she tried to run back out but ended up flipping over the table.

"I'mma kill that nigga. Meech, if you don't come get this bitch I'mma cook her ass for dinner. Tiger a le mode all in this bitch. You get a leg, you get a leg, bitch everybody gone get a fucking leg. Gone bitch, I don't wanna play with yo ass." Lana was trying to lick her and I could see the tears in my mama's eyes. She was scared as shit, but it was no way I was getting down to help her ass.

"Why the fuck you talking to yo grandchild like that Talia? She trying to bond and you in here cursing her out and shit like that shit don't bother her." Meech was dead serious, until he heard Lana growling. My mama looked at him and he knew shit was about to go bad. "Ma for real, don't hurt her. She just playing." My mama looked at him and threw daggers getting up. She knew he was really trying to save his pussy because he never called her ma.

"Why the fuck are you walking around with this mufucka?" Meech pulled out a stack of money and gave her this weird ass smile.

"Cus I need you to baby sit her while we go to the club tonight. Before you say no, think about how you do everything for this cry baby ass nigga and I never ask you for nothing. I don't trust her being alone right now and I really don't want you unprotected either." This nigga was laying it on thick and I could tell my mama was going for it.

"Put that bitch in the garage. If she even look at me funny, you gone come home to that bitch on the grill." Meech walked off to take her to the back and Mega walked in. You could tell he wasn't excited about this party at all. Either that or he was depressed about turning thirty.

"Nigga you good? You in this mufucka looking like you ready to go to sleep or some shit." When he shrugged, I knew he really wasn't trying to go.

"Something eating at me telling me to sit this one out. Shit don't feel right out here partying and the nigga that shot you and stole our bread still walking the streets." I felt where he was coming from, because I felt the same.

"I know, but yo brother went all out for this shit, so we gotta go. You only turn thirty once." Meech walked up and we stood to go. As soon as we got outside, Meech's phone rung.

"What up? Yeah, bet up." His ass hung up the phone and was excited as hell. "I got one of our nigga's sitting outside of Dream's house. I been making sure she was good and he said this nigga Shawn just went in her house. Shorty not there, she went to the club early to set up, so this is the perfect time to get his hoe ass." I was confused.

"How he know Dream?"

"Carl said it looked like he was sneaking in, so I guess they was trying to come after our bitches. Now are you going to keep asking questions, or do you wanna go get this nigga that got you out here looking like old ass gym socks. Holes all in yo shit. Bring ya ass leaky." Even though I was gritting on him, I jumped in the car because I wanted that nigga bad.

"Hey bro, I sholl hope you still keep your tool kit in the trunk." Meech laughed and nodded.

"Fuck yeah, you just never know." They had no idea, but I was so ready to see this nigga I was damn near about to explode. When we pulled up, we jumped out quick as hell and went to the trunk. Grabbing some more guns and the tool kit, we walked up to Dream's house quiet as hell.

"Before we go in, I just want to say this some sprung shit. You putting security on a bitch you swear you don't like." He gave me a death look and I laughed. "I'm just saying." Easing inside, we tried our best not to make no noise. This nigga was in the front room pacing back and forth. Raising my gun, I pointed it at him waiting on him to notice we were there.

"What the fuck?"

"Same thing I was saying when you shot me and left me for dead. Before I return the favor, I'mma need you to tell me where our bread at."

"Before you try to lie, we already know it was you. It don't even matter why at this point, but I will make this shit long and drawn out if you don't tell me where my shit at." Mega was making sure he understood he had no choice but to tell us.

"I didn't want to do none of the shit. I know yall won't believe me, but he was threatening to kill my sisters and I didn't know what else to do." Meech started unpacking the tools and Shawn's eyes got big as hell.

"You shot my brother, took our money, now you after our bitches. I'm sure you don't want to play this game."

"I didn't go after yo bitch, she came at me. Yeah, we fucked but she not worth me dying." You could see Meech was pissed.

"Who bitch? You ain't fuck my shorty, his girl the one that's a hoe. Who you fuck? I swear if you say my bitch name, I'mma pour acid in yo dick hole."

"Dreika." I couldn't believe that bitch.

"Oh, we already knew she was a hoe. Back to my bread. Where my shit at?" When he saw that it really was some acid, he started panicking.

"I was gone give it back to yall, that's why I never gave it to Lenox. My sisters are holding it for me." This shit was easier than I thought. Shawn wasn't really about this life and I felt bad that I was gone have to kill his ass.

"Who the fuck are your sisters and where they live?"

"Please don't hurt them." Meech walked over to him with the acid and Shawn panicked again. Brielle and Dream. We're in Dream's house, but the bread not here." We all looked at each other and I could tell my brothers was devastated. Especially Mega. Grabbing some rope and handcuffs, Meech started tying him up, so we joined in and helped.

"Nigga if you lying, I promise the shit not gone work out for you." It was so much venom in Mega's voice, the nigga scared me. I felt bad for him though. They joked about that shit with me, and I took it, but Meech would never let another bitch in. Once we knew he was secure, we jumped in the car and headed to Mega's building. Nobody said shit the entire way there.

When we got out, them niggas was on a mission. I could tell they prayed he was lying, but I knew he wasn't. Lenox had gotten to all of our girls and we fell for the bullshit.

As soon as we got to her door, Mega kicked the bitch in and we started looking around. These mufuckas didn't even try to hide the money. The shit was just sitting in her closets. After we got all our shit out, we got back in the car.

"Drive me to the club. I'm about to kill this bitch." Doing what Mega asked, Meech pulled off. At least the party hadn't started yet and it wouldn't be many witnesses. The way this nigga was driving, I prayed we got there in one piece. Not caring about shit else, them niggas barely parked and jumped out. As soon as we stepped inside, Mega started screaming. Brielle and Dream was looking confused as hell.

"YOU THINK YOU CAN STEAL FROM ME BITCH?" Before she could answer, shots rang out and I dove behind the bar. Them bitches was too close and I knew they were coming from inside the club. I was kicking my own ass for leaving my gun in the car. My brothers was gone talk big shit about me leaving them in a gun fight, but it wasn't shit I could do. Fuck was I gone do, throw a beer bottle at the shooters? The shots

finally stopped and I eased up from the bar to look around.

It was bodies sprawled out and my stomach dropped.

Stepping over the workers that was in there setting up, I

looked over at my brothers and they were sprawled out. Their

bodies was riddled in bullets and anyone else that was in

there was dead as well. There was no sign of Brielle and

Dream and all I could do was drop to my knees screaming.

TALIA...

"Maine, did you let that lil bitch out of the garage?"

"Naw man and why the fuck you worried about that pussy you need to worry about me tearing yo shit up. Stop trying to get out of giving me head and suck this mufucka."

"If you ain't let her out, then how the fuck is this lil bitch on the side of the bed looking at me swallow ya dick?" When I said that, he looked up and tried to jump out of the bed. I knew this mufucka was off, but I ain't know she was a damn pervert too. Grabbing my pillow, I swung it at her ass and kept trying to get her to move away. This bitch laid down on the floor like she was unbothered. "I swear one of these days I'mma sell yo ass to the circus."

"Get off that gay shit playing with that pussy and come back to this dick. If she wants to watch, let her." His ass was talking big shit for a mufucka that just jumped out the bed like a hoe. He barely had his whole ass on the bed. Nigga was leaning in on one cheek.

"If she bite me, I'mma fuck you up Maine. This shit ain't right." He looked at me like I was crazy.

"Do you want to tell her to get the fuck out? Okay then. Bring yo ass here and stop looking at her." Doing as he said, I came to his side of the bed and tried to concentrate, but I couldn't get my mind right. Lana was growling and made me feel like she was ready to attack. I think I scraped his dick one too many times and his ass was over it.

"Bend the fuck over man." Laughing, I did what I was told and he slid inside of me. Maine started going to work, but I was trying to find out why this lil hoe was crying and growling. If she thought she was gone get my man, she had me fucked up. Maine must have realized I wasn't paying attention, because he slapped me in the back of the head, but tried to play it off like he was trying to grab my hair.

"Nigga you tried it. Hit me again, I'll lock these muscles down on this cat and break that bitch." His ass laughed, but he knew I was dead ass serious. I'm guessing he couldn't take the crying either, because his ass came quick as hell. Normally, his ass would beat this shit up for hours and I would let him. Both of us was trying to figure out what the fuck was wrong with this lil hoe. "You want some meat don't you? Yo daddy over there feeding you grass, but baby want a steak don't she?" I was trying to talk nice to the hoe, so I could get around her. I didn't know how to act when she walked up on me and just rubbed against my leg whimpering.

She followed me into the kitchen, and I went in the fridge and grabbed some meat out of it. When I tried to give it to her, she turned away and kept crying. I ain't never like the lil hoe, but I felt bad that something was wrong with her. I didn't know what to do, so I just rubbed her head and tried to comfort her. Right as she started moaning harder, my phone rang. Seeing that it was Marco, I picked up.

"Hey son, shouldn't y'all be partying by now?" Looking

down, it looked like Lana was trying to listen to my

conversation, she was staring at me hard as hell and it had me

feeling a lil nervous.

"Ma, you need to get to the hospital right now.

Someone shot up the club and Mega and Meech... They, they.

Ma, you need to hurry up and get here." My heart sank and I

started screaming. As soon as I did, Lana started rubbing

against me again. I think that's what was wrong with her. She

was trying to tell me something was wrong with my son.

Maine came walking in the kitchen calm as hell.

"Woman, quit being scared of that damn cat. Just put

her back in the garage." When he saw that I was crying, he

rushed over to me. "What's wrong Talia?"

"Something happened to our sons. We need to get to

the hospital now." Shaking off that weak bitch shit, I ran

towards the bathroom and did a quick hoe bath. Throwing on

my clothes, I grabbed my gun and walked in the front room.

Maine was already waiting on me and we went out the door. The drive to the hospital was quiet and my nerves were on a thousand. I had no idea how bad it was and that was what was bothering me the most. Maine barely had the car stopped when I jumped out and ran inside. Marco was standing there pacing and the look on his face told me it was bad. As soon as he saw me, he ran to my arms and broke down.

"Ma, they had so many holes in them. It was bad and I couldn't help them." Wiping my eyes, I walked over to the counter and slammed my gun down getting the nurse's attention.

"Find me somebody to come out here and tell me what the fuck is going on with my sons, or I will tear this bitch up. You got five fucking minutes. Tic Toc bitch." Looking at my watch, the nurse grabbed the phone and started making calls. Four minutes later, a doctor walked out towards us.

"I know that this is scary, but I need you to let us work on your sons. All I can tell you right now is to prepare yourselves. It is not looking good, but we are doing everything we can. I'm not sure if it's much more we can do, it was too much blood loss and the bullets tore through them, but we will keep trying." He walked off and my body started shaking. Somebody thought it was okay to take out my sons, my muthafuckin' sons and wasn't shit gone happen. Walking over to Maine, I snapped off.

"I don't want to hear yo shit. We have to come the fuck out of retirement. They do not get away with this. It's time to make the city bleed." He nodded and looked at me.

"We gone need more than us to go to war. No offense, but I'mma need more security than Marco." I wanted to laugh, but my baby looked offended.

"You are the only one not shot, which tells me yo ass booked it son. It's okay, I'm just gone call in a lil more help." Grabbing my phone, I made a few calls. Once I was done, I sat down with my family waiting to hear anymore news. My heart was hurting, but I didn't have time to be a weak bitch. I had to finish this shit for my babies and that's what the fuck I was going to do. A few hours later, we were still waiting.

"I'm just curious, who the fuck did you call for back up?" Before I could respond, they walked in acting a fucking fool.

"I know damn well ain't nobody done fucked with my family! Ion know bout y'all but Lai with all the bullshit tunight. If a war is what these bitch niggas want, a war is what the fuck they gone get. Lai here baby point me to the nearest bitch nigga so my bullets can play with they muthafuckin tonsils." My cousin Lai came in the hospital raising hell, but what took me out is the shirt she was wearing. It said 'Bitch niggas gone be some slumpt niggas.

"Who need pussy on they tonsils? I got pussy for days and I'm ready to fuck a nigga to they meet they maker. I mean, fuck em up. Damn boy, you sholl done grown up. Come here and give Aunnie a kiss on this crouching tiger."

Before I could say anything, Maine looked at me and I shook my head.

"No the fuck you didn't call Ma Lai and Debra Hoover."

"Yes the fuck I did."

TO BE CONT...

Get connected with Author K. Renee

To get VIP access of new releases, and sneak peeks please join my mailing list.

Text KRENEE to 22828

Website www.authorkrenee.com

Facebook: https://www.facebook.com/karen.renee.9421450

Instagram: http://www.instagram.com/Authorkrenee

KEEP UP WITH LATOYA NICOLE

Like my author page on fb @misslatoyanicole

My fb page Latoya Nicole Williams

IG Latoyanicole35

Twitter Latoyanicole35

Snap Chat iamTOYS

Reading group: Toy's House of Books

Email latoyanicole@yahoo.com

Other Books by K. Renee

Loved by A Billionaire- The Kassom Brothers 1-3

A Boss Saved Me 1-2

A Real One Captured My Heart 1-3

Loved by A Billionaire – Ma Lai

His Love Was Law 1-2

The Billionaire's Daughter 1-2

OTHER BOOKS BY LATOYA NICOLE (AVAILABLE ON AMAZON)

NO WAY OUT: MEMOIRS OF A HUSTLA'S GIRL 1-2

GANGSTA'S PARADISE 1-2

ADDICTED TO HIS PAIN (STANDALONE)

LOVE AND WAR: A HOOVER GANG AFFAIR 1-4

CREEPING WITH THE ENEMY: A SAVAGE STOLE MY HEART PART 1-2

I GOTTA BE THE ONE YOU LOVE (STANDALONE)

THE RISE AND FALL OF A CRIME GOD: PHANTOM AND ZARIA'S STORY 1-2

ON THE 12TH DAY OF CHRISTMAS MY SAVAGE GAVE TO ME

A CRAZY KIND OF LOVE: PHANTOM AND ZARIA

14 REASONS TO LOVE YOU: A LATOYA NICOLE ANTHOLOGY

SHADOW OF A GANGSTA

THAT GUTTA LOVE 1-2

LOCKED DOWN BY HOOD LOVE 1-2

THE BEARD GANG CHRONICLES 2 (THE TEASE)

THROUGH THE FIRE: A STANDALONE NOVEL

DAUGHTER OF A HOOD LEGEND 1-2

CRAVING THE LOVE OF A THUG 1-2

SON OF A CRIME GOD, DAUGHTER OF A HOOVER 1-3

SON OF A CRIME GOD, DAUGHTER OF A HOOVER THE WEDDING

MADE TO LOVE YOU (NOVELLA)

CPSIA information can be obtained
at www.ICGtesting.com
Printed in the USA
LVHW021548061120
670969LV00010B/846